Winter's Wonderland

CHERYL BARTON

Dear Reader,

I know that we are in trying times that tend to impact our mental and emotional stability, let alone one of a financial nature. As a writer of romance, I enjoy bringing you stories that, hopefully, allows you to step away from every bit of negativity that is slowing you down and bringing you down and into a world of peace, love and happiness.

I believe in happily ever after. Know that whatever you are going through this too shall pass. The meantime, I want to introduce you to Winter and Dante. They were married and then life happened. If you know my books, you know that absolutely believe in love a second time around, rekindled romance and yes, second and third chances at love. Winter missed her wonderland where she would play until her heart and her body were satisfied. She's back at it again. Dante is more than ready to oblige what he walked away from. It's the love in the end that truly matters.

Grab your favorite drink, a little snacky-snack and indulge in this sexy romance. It's all about the love!

Thanks for always supporting me. I appreciate you!

Cheryl

About the Author

Cheryl Barton is the author of over sixty romance and inspirational novels. In her spare time, she enjoys traveling, reading crime, espionage and sci-fi novels, watching classic movies and television shows, making wreaths, time spent with family and friends and indulging in Maryland steamed crabs. Connect with Cheryl on Facebook, Instagram, Threads and TikTok. You can find links to her social media accounts at www.cherylbarton.net.

Check out the complete listing of Cheryl's books!

Romance Series'

Island Embers
Hunger for You
Desire for You
Thirst for You

The Brothers of Chi-Town
I Can't Let Go
Swagger and Baggage
Claiming His Child
Always Bet on Black
It Takes Two to Tangle
Crashing into Love
Leaks, Lies, Lust and Love
Love's Gamble

The Sullivans of Montana
Home for Thanksgiving
The Way You Love Me
On the Right Track
Three's a Crowd
The Law of Love

Sister Act
An Unexpected Destiny
For You, I Will
More than Friends

A Lovers' Heart
Heartthrob
Heartbeat
Heartbreaker

Second Chances
Snowbound
Cupid's Arrow
One Wish

Bachelor Series
Bachelor Not for Sale
A Designed Affair
A Perfect Combination
Love at Last

Amorous Occupations
The Artist
The Bookkeeper
The Chef
The Dancer
The Electrician
The Gambler (2026)
The First Baseman (2027)

Sweet Things
The Sweetest Temptation
The Sweetest Revenge

Romance Standalone

Never Can Say Goodbye
The Diner
It Should Have Been You
The Christmas Layover
Love Therapy
Mister Christmas
The Power of Seduction
A Christmas Wish
Being Neighborly
Seize the Moment
Baby, Come Back
Unforgettable
One Moment in Time
Dashing Through the Snow
True Lies or True Love
A Trick and a Treat
When I Think of You
The Lake House

Love at First Sight
Take a Knee
My First Love
Love on Top
His Halloween Promise
Bossy
Holly for Christmas
And Then There Was You
Un-break My Heart
A Better Man
Winter's Wonderland
His Holiday Wife (2025)
Playing for Keeps (2026)
Girls Trippin' (2026)
The Real Deal (2026)

Inspirational Series'

When God Says Yes
Rescue Me
Release Me
Restore Me (July 2026)

Dad's Matter
Girl Dad, 1
Girl Dad, 2 (June 2026)

Encouraging Words from
One Sister to Another
One Sister Away (Vols 1—4)
On Sister Away, Vol. 5
(2026)

Inspirational Standalone

Breaking Chains: Down, But
Not Out
A Letter to My Mother
Straightening Her Crown

Urban Drama Standalone

Amerikka: Justice or Revenge
(Dec. 2025)

Urban Drama/Romance Series

Straight Outta Baltimore
Seven Days, book 1 (2026)
Six Relays, book 2 (2026)

2026 New Romance Series

House of Cards
Ace of Spades
King of Clubs
Queen of Diamonds
Jack of Hearts

Family Drama Series

New 12-Book Series
Begins September 2026

Divas of High Hill – The Series

Prequel - The Come Up: The
Rise of Tyrus Hill (09/2026)
Secrets, Book 1 (09/2026)
Pillow Talk, Book 2
(12/2026)
Scandalous, Book 3
(04/2027)

*Upcoming books italicize

One

"Winter, it's been two years."

"And?"

Somewhere on her sofa, Winter Shaw could hear her phone ringing. It was faint, so it had to be between the cushions. After the second ring and her inability to get her hand on it, she hopped up off of the L-shaped red sectional and began tossing the pillows onto the floor behind her. First there was a red one, then a gold one and last, a mint green one. Behind her she heard chuckles of laughter and frustration.

"Girl, stop it! You're hitting me!"

Winter smothered her giggles with one hand when she looked up and found that when she tossed the pillows, they were landing in the face and with body assaults on her best friend, Davina Washington. Winter found it comical that she was attacking the plush pillows by quickly somersaulting them back up on the chair on the opposite end.

Seeing the bright orange iPhone case, Winter grabbed her phone before it finished ringing.

"Hello?" she said.

"Yes, I'm looking for Winter Shaw?" the caller asked.

Out of breath, Winter plopped down on the other end of

the sofa between the pillows, playfully moving Davina out of the way.

"This is Winter Shaw."

Winter put the phone on speaker as she fixed the pillows.

"Ms. Shaw, my name is Rhea McDonald. I'm calling on behalf of the house you were looking to reserve for the month of December in Ridgway, Colorado. You inquired about the availability?"

Winter paused before replying. She tried to recall what the caller was referencing. In a few seconds, she remembered.

"Oh, yes. I did. I completely forgot about that."

"Are you still interested in the house? It's available."

"Um, yes, I am."

"I'm new here, but Ms. Battle explained to me that you were familiar with the property."

"Is Rocki not available?"

"No, she isn't. I'm sorry. She is on maternity leave. Her baby came early. I'm taking over her properties while she's out."

"Wow! That's amazing to hear. She's almost a month early. Are she and the baby okay?"

"Yes. They are doing great. She had the baby about two weeks ago. She and her daughter are doing wonderfully. We expect pictures later this week. She left me specific instructions by email last night to let you know the house was available and would be ready for you on December first if you still want it. The owner still has it listed to be rented. We've had a few inquiries about it. I was told to give you first pick."

Winter grinned like she'd just won the lottery. She couldn't see her own smile but she felt how wide her cheeks were spread and showing all of her teeth.

"Oh, that's wonderful. I didn't hear anything back when I called two weeks ago. I know there is still time since it's only September."

Winter couldn't believe her luck.

"Great. There have been a few upgrades. Again, I understand you've been to this house before."

Winter looked over at Davina who was mouthing something that she couldn't make out. Taking the phone off of the speaker, she moved to her favorite corner of the chair and crossed her socked covered feet under her.

"Yes. My hus...ex-husband and I owned the property a few years back. He owns it outright now. I was told by a friend that he puts it on the rental list for most months, especially the winter months."

"Yes. It's open for the month you want. We also have one week in January and one month in February still available. The house is booked for October and November. It's never rented the last three days of the month to allow us to inspect and restock supplies and for deep cleaning. That would mean your rental period would end on December twenty-eighth. Is that okay for you?"

"It is. You mentioned upgrades?"

"There is a new Jacuzzi on the new deck that was installed back in the summer. The owner also added two extra bedrooms and two bathrooms; one bed and bath on the second floor and the same on the first floor."

"That's big. That means it has four bedrooms and four bathrooms now."

"Four and a half. There is still a powder room on the entry level. There is also an additional fireplace and the kitchen was completely remodeled to double the original size. There are a

3

few smaller upgrades like a larger pantry and some new flooring. Since Mr. Eastman opened it back up for rentals, it's pretty much booked up for months ahead of schedule. Should I lock this in for you?"

"Can you tell me what the cost is for the time I'll be there?"

"It's seven thousand for the month."

"That sounds great. I'll take it."

"Okay. I'm going to email you the registration link. Will there be any other guests for the month?"

"No. It'll just be me."

"It's a mighty big house for one person. You'll be fine, I'm sure. I almost forgot to mention that the alarm system has been upgraded to a top-of-the-line model. Once I have your registration and payment, I'll reconnect with you to go over everything."

"I'll get it all back to you today, if you send it before seven or eight this evening. Otherwise, I'll get to it tomorrow morning; first thing."

"Oh, no rush. I will have it locked in for you as long as I have everything by mid-October. I'll be sending you a lot of information. Since you know a lot about the house having been one of the owners at one point, I won't go as deep into the weeds about every little thing that the house offers. Feel free to ask me any questions at any time. I'll get everything out to you shortly."

"Thank you for letting me know it's available. I'm already excited to see the upgrades. I haven't been there in two years."

"You're welcome, Ms. Shaw. Have a great day."

Winter threw her phone back into the pillows and bounced up and down more energized than she had been before the call.

"I'm going to Colorado!" she declared.

"You're what? Did I just hear you say that you're going to Colorado for a month? Not only that, but you're staying at the house you used to own with Dante?"

"Yes. What's wrong with that? I love that house."

"I know you did."

"I still do love it. It's a perfect getaway location. You've been there. You know how gorgeous it is surrounded by all of those snow-covered mountains. It's a beautiful house. There have been a lot of upgrades that I can't wait to see."

Then there was dead air. Winter and Davina looked at each other and communicated without words. That's how friendships of over twenty years work.

"Let me see if I have this right. You are the creator, writer, producer and director of the hottest show streaming these days. The show won five Emmy's, including best director for you. The hype for season two is off the chain. Every news and social media platform, including network television, is trying to interview you about how successful the show is. *Girl's Trippin'* is a hit. You get to take a month off? "

"Two months would be more like it. I need this time to rejuvenate my mind, body and soul."

"You are living the life! The studio isn't looking for the next big hit from you while also expecting season two of the show to be as big as season one?" Davina asked.

"That's a reason I'm taking the time off. I'm actually taking one month at the cabin and then a month to visit my family in Baltimore. I was going to go see them for November but changed my mind. I haven't seen my parents or my sister and her family in over a year. I need the time off. I've been on skates for two years working, writing and producing. I need a break."

"Why the Colorado house? You can afford to go anywhere. What about a beach resort? A quiet island where a bikini is the attire for the day? You're weird. You're going to one of the coldest places in the heart of the winter. That makes no sense to me."

"Because I love it and I miss it. Besides, I live in Los Angeles. I can wear a bikini any time. You live here too. Don't you yearn for colder temperatures sometime? It'll be Christmas time. It's supposed to be ice cold and snowy."

Winter chuckled when Davina shook her head so hard from side to side that she thought any minute, it would fly off of her body.

"I hate the cold. I was meant for hot beaches that are full of hot men. Is this about missing Dante?"

Winter shrugged her shoulders and avoided eye contact.

"Maybe. Perhaps just a little bit. He won't be there. If the house is available, it means he's probably on the road. He doesn't usually go to the house until the warmer months. The extreme cold bothers his leg."

"You've talked to him."

"No. Not for some time now. One of his friends is going through something medically serious. I called Dante to see how he was handling the crisis his friend is going through. That was a few months ago."

"How do you know so much about where he is and when?"

"Ms. Ida Mae. His mother and I stay in contact. Thought, not as much as when I was married to Dante, but I keep up on how she's doing her. Once she moved into the senior community in Orlando, Florida, I check in on her after she left Los Angeles."

"And you can't check in with her without checking up on him? Why would you care?"

"Davina, don't start with me. I was married to him for eight years."

"And he dumped you like you never meant anything to him."

They both almost leaped off of the sofa when heavy rain slammed into the large window panes of Winter's twentieth floor, corner condominium, followed by loud thunder and sky sparkling lightning.

"That was loud," Winter acknowledged.

"I don't know how you can live up this high. Nothing over the seventh floor for me. Did you know that the ladder on a fire truck doesn't go higher than that? I prefer when you lived in your house in the Hollywood Hills."

"I love it here. As for Dante, that's not fair. I don't know why you and the girls keep bringing that up."

"We don't understand why you don't bring it up enough."

"I easily talk about it plenty," Winter answered confidently.

"Is that so? Let's check into that."

When Davina took out her phone, Winter tried to stop her by reaching for it, but she moved out of reach as the phone, on speaker, began to ring.

"I wish you wouldn't," she pleaded.

Winter knew what was coming next. She felt like she was being set up for this call. The gabfest that she hated was about to take place.

"Hey Vina!"

"Josie. Hold on while I connect Tachina. I'm here at Winter's place."

"Davina, no," Winter tried to whisper.

"I heard that. You don't want to talk to us?" Josie said.

"I love y'all," Winter exclaimed.

"Did I hear Winter's voice?" Tachina chimed in.

"You did. I'm here at Winter's place and guess what?"

"What?" Tachina and Josie said at the same time.

"She's spending a month at the house in Colorado."

"With Dante?" Josie asked.

"No. He won't be there."

"Whew. That's a good thing. We told you to leave that man alone. The way he disrespected you does not warrant you giving him even a single brain cell of thought," Tachina added.

"Now is not the time to come for me about this. His life changed drastically after the shooting and the fire. He was devastated with having to leave the force," Winter tried to explain to them for the millionth time.

"No, you are not defending a man who dropped you faster than a hot plate. You stuck by him for almost a year after that happened. In the end, he said thanks for the help, but no thanks to the marriage," Davina chimed in.

"Spare me your judgment. I don't want to hear it. I was married to him. None of you have been married. You don't know what that was like."

"No, you didn't!" Tachina yelled.

"I'm not being disrespectful of your life choices as if being single is something to look down on. I'm simply stating that you know me, but you don't know my entire situation with Dante. Besides, he won't be there. I want to get away for a while to work on some new showrunner ideas. I love snow and Colorado has a lot of it. All of you are from the west coast. I come from Maryland where we got snow."

"Are you going for nostalgia reasons? Like, a place to go to reminisce about what your life was life being married and being in that cabin with him?" Josie asked.

"I'm going because... Listen, I'm not going to continue to explain the decisions I make as a grown woman. I'm going and that's the end of it. Dante won't be there. Don't start another barrage of reasons why I should never think about Dante Eastman again. Give it a rest. Now, I'm going to step out of the room and if Davina wants to continue the conversation, you all can do that. I'm done. I'm okay if we stop having these powwows only to pile on me. Got it?" Winter asked.

Any other time, she would handle the playful banter about her life from her friends, but not today. Her purpose right now was to find her peace. She loved her friends but having them in her ear all the time about the state of her then marriage was not where she wanted to be today. Having to listen to them criticize her life for the past two years was enough.

Winter walked into her living room and sat down on the long white sofa. She rested her feet up on the large soft, round ottoman. She had a perfect view of the Los Angeles skyline. Going to the house in Colorado had her thinking of a time when she was at her happiest.

Back when she was married, she and Dante would steal time away to shut out the world. She worked as a busy executive while he served as a captain and the lead for one of the Los Angeles S.W.A.T. teams. He did so until that fateful day when he was injured in the line of duty. The house in Colorado was the second house purchase they made as a couple. Dante had friends who lived there year-round. He would visit them often and loved the area. She was sold when he approached her about having a place there instead of always staying at a hotel or a lodge. Life was good there and here in Los Angeles until one night on his job almost cost him his life. Little did she know that the incident would also lead to the downfall of her marriage. It took her a long time to recover. Now that she had, as well as moved on, she could go back to the house that meant so much to her and enjoy it in peace. The only difference this time is, she was going without Dante. She wondered how he was really doing.

The last time she saw him in person was the day she signed the final divorce papers in her attorney's office. They said their final silent farewell and went in two different directions. Later that night when she returned home, she cried over not just the loss of her marriage but over the man she once knew before he turned into the cold, hard, asshole that struggled to walk away using a cane to balance the fact that he still had a hard time walking without the help on his left side.

More than physical damage to his body, Dante was also damaged by an ego that consumed him to the point where he could no longer face a life with her. That made her sad. Out of that, she finally had to realize that he chose what worked best for him and not them, good or bad. She had to let him have that. She was forced to go on with her life as a single woman again. After all that he had taken her through, she still wished him well. She still loved him.

Out of nowhere, a glass a wine appeared in her face. Davina was shoving it at her as a peace offering.

"Are you mad at me?" Davina questioned.

Winter looked her way and with soft eyes, invited her to join her on the sofa by moving over and making room for her.

"No. I know what you and the girls are trying to do. You can't help me. What you need to stop doing is beating me up because I wanted to fight for my marriage; for my man. You can't bring up all the negatives every time his name may come up. I love all three of you. I listened to you and I walked away from my marriage without looking back; without fighting harder."

Davina leaned back and placed her hand over her heart. "You blame us?"

"Kill the drama, please. No, not for that. I blame you for not having my back. Instead, you all badgered me and slammed him to no end. You weren't fair. I know you felt your way because of how he treated me at that time. What we all forgot was before that, there were amazing years with him."

"Sis, we didn't forget about that; Dante did. I'm sorry for calling the girls. I honestly didn't think it would make you angry at us. I know your life is hectic. I want you to take your trip and have a great time shopping so that you can bring me something back. Most of all, I want you to have the peace you've been chasing. We both know that with the kind of work you do that demands so much of your time, you haven't been able to enjoy it much; not the way you would like. You're still wounded from the death of your marriage. Do what you need to do. If you need me – if you need *us*, you know how to reach us."

Winter locked her arms with Davina. She laid her head on Davina's shoulder.

"I'm supposed to still be a wife. I was supposed to have started my journey as a mother by now. I'm thirty-three. In order to have that again, I have to start over. I was so focused on my career that I didn't think that there was a possibility that I would have time to have babies with Dante. I really wanted that."

"Don't worry about that right now. Go spend your time in Colorado where you can write and rest. In the snow they get there, you won't have to worry about doing much else."

"That's the plan. That is always the plan."

"Besides, Dante is probably in his trailer thing somewhere down south. Out of sight means out of mind. There is no need for any of us to bring him up because like you said, he will be nowhere around. You'll have a happy Christmas not thinking about that name at all. We good?" Davina asked.

"You're right. No need at all. Just me spending Christmas alone in the snow while writing the next big Hollywood hit."

Winter said that more for Davina's benefit than hers. She wasn't ready to tell her friend or anyone else that being in a place where she and Dante loved each other all up, down and around the cabin was sure to keep her mind and her sexually-starve body thinking about him. Winter in Colorado to the left, she thought. If all she did for a month was think about hot nights from her past with Dante, she could think of worse things she could be thinking about.

Two

Making his way to one of the coldest parts of the country, Colorado, is not where Dante Eastman thought he'd find himself. On the first day of December. His original plan for the upcoming holiday month was to drive his Ford F-450 super duty truck which was pulling the Airstream Classic 33FB Twin with Solar and Lithium Package fifth wheel that he'd purchased over a year ago to Florida to spend time with his mother. Ida Mae Eastman, he knew, was looking forward to his visit.

After starting out on this new path in life, though a lonely one, he had purchased it in order to travel the country. He'd thought about doing so plenty of times in the past, but never actually did it until his divorce two years ago from a woman he didn't spend enough time appreciating. Getting the trailer, he discovered that he loved the outdoors, no matter the weather. Most of all, he enjoyed camping out in it. He loved the carefree life. There was a lot of time to reflect. His biggest discovery was that at a time when he suffered a pity party, he should have been focusing on rebuilding his life with his wife; not without her. He's been living with that notion for almost two years. So far, there hasn't been an opportunity for them to be in the same place where he could talk to her about the mistake he made in breaking up their happy home. He needed a plan. If there was a way to get Winter back, he would do anything.

The only person he said that he wasn't happy in life without Winter was his mother. She had been in his corner all of his life. They'd grown even closer after his father died. Being an only child, another purpose in life for him was to look after and take care of her. She consistently told him that he was doing a great job with her. He needed to now work on getting his wife back. If he really thought that he could, he would. He wasn't still long enough in one place to even make an attempt. He needed time to think. Constantly being on the road provided ample time to think. For some reason, it wasn't working. He now had a new plan.

His mother must have known that she was on his mind. His phone rang and her face appeared on the video screen in the truck.

"Hey, Ma!"

"Dante Eastman! I am still upset with you for not coming here for Christmas."

He exhaled loudly. He knew that until he made his way to her, she would bring this up during every call between them.

"I know you're upset with me. I'm sorry. I promise I will be there in a few months."

"But you hate the cold weather. It's hell on your wounds. The warm weather here will do wonders for your continued progress toward walking just as you had before...well, before what happened took place. I haven't set eyes on you in months – not since you flew here back in July. It's December. I need to see my only son," she appealed.

He wondered if she was okay. If not, he would change his plan and hop on a plane to Florida.

"Is anything wrong? Are you okay? Is there an issue at your senior community?"

"No. Everything is wonderful. I was just bragging to Agnes, you know, the loud mouth of the community, that my wonderful son was coming for a visit. Now what am I going to brag about? She'll have a field day."

"Ma, your sisters and your best friend, JoAnne are all coming to see you for the holiday. I would be a fifth wheel. You'll have a great time. I'm still sending a caterer for the holiday party you want to have in your condo. The holiday decorator will be there next week to decorate your place the way you want. I know it's not the same, but I hope you will understand that I just want to have a quiet, relaxed Christmas this year at the house in Colorado. I haven't been since the final upgrades were made. I'd like to see everything."

"What about your leg? How is it doing?"

Dante rubbed his knee where the damage had been done by a bullet. Fragments were still left inside of him that were too small to remove.

"My leg is great. I'm still doing therapy. I don't use the came as much as I used to. I'm much better."

"But you're all over the place. Weren't you just in Seattle visiting Zane? All this traveling around and time behind the wheel can't be good on your leg."

"No. I was in Texas. Booker, from my old S.W.A.T. unit has taken a turn for the worse. I think I told you that he was diagnosed with prostate cancer. The cancer has spread to his liver and metastasized to other parts of his body. He has decided to end all treatment and spend the time he has left with his family and friends."

"Oh, my. I didn't know. I'm sorry to hear that. I know how close the two of you are. I remember when he came with you to visit me a few times some years ago. How is his wife doing? I don't remember her name."

"It's Cynthia. She's holding on strong. Some of her family was there to help her with him. They moved to Texas to be near his family, which was a great idea. They have a large village. Their kids are still trying to process what's going on. They're still pretty young. I wanted to spend some time with him. We did a lot of catching up and reliving the good days together on S.W.A.T."

Thinking about Booker, who turned out to be one of his best friends, reminded him what he missed about being married to Winter. Yes, he missed being a S.W.A.T. officer but most of all, he missed being a husband. Nothing topped that. Not even the day he said goodbye to S.W.A.T. Though his commander had offered him a position at headquarters that would allow him to still be a S.W.A.T. officer, he turned it down because he couldn't see himself not out in the field. Time with Booker added to his revelations over the past few years that the life they had there wasn't everything. It was the family that made their houses a home at the end of the day.

"I know you miss those days. This trek around the country in your camper is nice but one day, what will you do when it's no longer enough? You know I would love it if you moved closer to me. With your father gone, I can't say I'm lonely because I'm not. I have a full life. I worry about you."

"I'm good. I promise I am. I wouldn't lie to you about that. We've been through too much as mother and son for me to sugarcoat anything with you. Seeing Booker did something to me. I have a lot to think through."

"And feel sorry for yourself about? I know you're second-guessing some things. I think she is too."

He knew who she was talking about. He wasn't ready to have that conversation.

"Mom, I know you still stay in contact with Winter. I love that for you and her. I can't get into a conversation about her with you, right now. What you want for us is over. I really messed that up. I'm sure she's moved on. Even if she hasn't and you know, don't reveal anything the two of you talk about. She confides in you because she loves you. She also knows you can be a vault. It's why we both trust you with our secrets. I'm sorry I won't make it there for the holidays. If there is anything else you want, outside of me visiting right now, let me know. I got you."

"You take great care of me. Your father knew he wouldn't have anything to worry about leaving me over the same reason your friend is currently going through; cancer. When he slept away from here, his last words were that he could die peacefully knowing that I would never want for anything because I would always have you."

A slight lump formed in Dante's throat. His father has been gone for six years. There wasn't a day that went by that he didn't think about him. This time of year was especially hard. His father loved the Thanksgiving to Christmas holiday season. They were a small immediate family but their extended family was huge. They would all gather in Florida at what was his childhood home growing up to celebrate big for both holidays.

His father also loved his ex-wife. Winter was the daughter they never had but always wanted. Even though they are divorced, he appreciated that she checked in on his mother several times a month.

"Ma, you will always have me. I think I need to spend this time here in Colorado. I'm sending you something special for Christmas. I'll also video chat with you on Christmas morning like we've done so many times. I love you. Look, Zane is calling in."

"Okay. Tell him I said hello. Have you seen your godchildren lately?"

Dante looked to the passenger side dashboard where he kept photos of family and friends. Zane Polson was his best friend since their childhood in Florida. He was married to another childhood friend, Maya and they had two children, Danny, their four-year-old son and Nakita, their two-year-old daughter. They were his godchildren. He adored them like crazy. They loved him like crazy.

"Only by video chat. I may fly there sometime next year."

"Okay. Go ahead and talk to Zane. Tell him I saw his mother in Miami when I went on that casino bus trip back in the summer."

"I will. Love you, Ma."

"Love you too, son. Call me after you get settled. Don't forget to send me new pictures of what the house looks like now. I know how much you love that house. Great memories?" she asked.

Dante nodded. The memories he held closest to his heart are those that included his time at the house with Winter.

"The greatest of memories," he finally said.

Ending the call, he called Zane back without bothering to listen to the voicemail he left.

"Bro!" Zane said the moment the call connected. "I just

finished leaving you a reasonable length message," he quipped.

"Hey! Good hearing from you."

"Is it? I called you twice in the past week and yet, I don't remember a call back. What's going on with you?"

Dante hesitated. His admission was going to garner a talk, like one with his mother, that he wasn't in the mood for. He took a baited breath before speaking.

"Nothing much. I'm on my way to Colorado. In fact, I'm about an hour away from the house."

"What happened to you parking that streamer of yours and flying out here to Seattle? I guess that's out now?"

"I never said I was going to do it. I told you I would think about it. I decided to have a quiet holiday at the house."

"Isn't it rented out this time of year? A lot of people love to spend this season in snowy Ridgway."

"So do I, just in case you forgot."

"You're usually there in the warmer months. You staying for the month? If not, the invitation is still open to spend Christmas with us unless you're heading to Florida."

"I'm not on both fronts. Thanks for the offer. Besides, you and Maya are two very busy surgeons who I am sure are not off for the holiday. Holiday seasons are usually your busiest. Listen, I get why everyone tries to convince me to spend the holiday season with them. Yes, I have not forgotten that Winter and I got married on Christmas Eve some eight years ago. My time at the house has nothing to do with her."

Dante loved his friends, but he hated that everyone thought that he was so fragile that when holidays came around, they needed to keep him from spending it alone. Yes, the shooting and subsequent fire damaged his body for good, but not his mind.

"We're worried about you. How is your leg? You know Maya wants to get a look at it."

"Your wife did an amazing job on my surgery. If it wasn't for her masterful hands, I may have lost my leg. Flying her in to Los Angeles when Winter called you was the best decision she's ever made."

"Besides loving and marrying you, of course!" Zane joked.

"Yeah, whatever. As I just said to my mother, I am fine. I'm doing good. The leg is good. I'll fly out after the holiday so that Maya can take a look at her work. She's helped me find therapist all over this country depending on where this F-450 takes me. I appreciate that. I'm about to pull the truck over and gas it up before getting to the house. I'll call the kids in a few days. Give them big hugs from their uncle Dante. Make sure you tell them that I love them. I sent them big packages for Christmas."

"We got them. Maya is going to damage your other leg for the drum set gift for Danny. What kind of friend sends their friend's kid a drum set?"

"The kind that doesn't live in the same house as his friend. Good luck with that!" he laughed. "I love them. Have fun putting that gigantic doll house together for Nakita."

"You are the worse best friend. One day, when you have kids, I will remember to return the favor."

Dante wasn't sure that day would come. He wanted that with Winter. No other woman crosses his mind when he thinks of being a father; only her.

"Give everyone my love."

"They love you too. So do I, bro."

"Ditto."

Pulling his truck with the streamer attached into the gas station lot, he hopped out and took out his phone again. Scrolling through, he clicked on the number that he'd tossed between calling and not calling for the past few months. Like then, he was still hesitant. Her beautiful face graced the screen. He still loved her. He still wanted her. His treatment of the woman who had once loved him unconditionally was a disgrace. He didn't even want to use the excuse that he was feeling sorry for himself and didn't want her to suffer a lifetime of taking care of him. He was a crippled man, in more than the physical way. He had burns on his body that he wanted to hide from the world, including her.

Being full of regret, he put the phone back in his pocket. She didn't need his apologies. Winter needed a life that didn't remind her that the man that had once vowed to love her through the good and the bad had lied. When things got bad, at their worse, he chose to walk away from her.

Yes. He was definitely full of regret.

Three

Winter rounded the bend and the house that she once loved more than her home in Los Angeles came into view. It was more beautiful than she had remembered. Not being here for over three years brought back nostalgic memories of many days and nights of being in love with the location and the man she's spent her time here with.

According to her friends, returning to the scene of the crime, their words, was the biggest mistake she could make. They didn't understand why she couldn't move on. She had enough money to buy her own house in the mountains. Yet, she chose to spend her money and time on renting out the same house that was once hers.

Winter happily gave up her stake in the house. When Dante offered to buy her out of it, she didn't want that. She loved the house, but not as much as he did. She wanted him to have it. She opted for their Los Angeles Hills home. She didn't even last long there. With the memories burning into her brain every day and night, she had to move out of it. When she did, she bought her current condo which was more fitting for her. Besides, she spent more time at the production studio in her office than she did at home.

Pulling up in front of the house, she took in the majesty that it was.

The white siding that covered brick on two sides was beautiful. The front was still all red-brick. Unless Dante covered the back, it looked the same as the front. The large wraparound porch was new. The last time she was here, there was a large porch in the front that didn't connect to the back deck. In the back, there was a large covered deck and patio. The woman from the property management company mentioned that there was a new jacuzzi. From the paperwork she received with pictures of the entire inside and outside of the house, the Jacuzzi was on the covered patio in back.

On the right side of the house, there was a new large open area. She could see a hookup and connection that was probably for Dante's streamer or any other guests who traveled by way of a trailer. There was also a connection to the house for an electric car, if someone had one.

She wondered if the other houses that were nearby still had the same owners. She and Dante would sometimes attend gatherings the neighbors had if they were in town. For this trip, she wanted to be left alone. Peace and quiet was the name of the game.

Getting out of the black Chevrolet Tahoe that she rented for her stay after landing at the airport, Winter walked up on the porch. She walked to both ends to look at more of the property. Dante had finally surrounded the back and sides of the house with a large privacy fence. They loved the animals that lived in the mountainous woods, but they once spoke of how close some would venture to the house.

Going back around to the front door, there was a lock box that contained the key and code to the front door. Taking off her gloves, she shivered against the cold that immediately hit her hands as she pulled her cell phone out of her jacket pocket.

She checked it for the code that was sent to her from the property management company. Entering it, the box didn't open. She tried it again. Nothing. After the third try, she knew it was time to make a call.

As soon as the phone rang, to her delight, she recognized Rhea's voice.

"Hello, this is Winter East..sorry, Winter Shaw. I'm at the house in Ridgway, Colorado that I'm renting for the month. The code you supplied me with to open the box doesn't work. I can't get the key or the code to the front door. Can you help me with that?"

"Oh, Ms. Shaw. I'm so sorry. I tried reaching you a few days ago. I left you several voice messages. There has been a mix up that I've been trying to remedy," Rhea tried to explain.

"A mix up? What kind of mix up?"

"The house wasn't supposed to be rented this month. The month of December had blackout dates. I wasn't looking at the right address on the calendar, though I was looking at the pictures of the house."

"Rhea, I don't understand. What's going on? I don't have the house for the month?"

"No. The good news is that I was able to find you another house a few miles away. The amenities are pretty much exactly the same. I didn't discover the issue until a week ago. I called you. I also sent you several emails."

Sadness immediately hit Winter like a raging storm. She was looking forward to staying at the house that was once hers, not some other house that didn't hold any memories for her. It's the memories that she was chasing, not just the location. Winter checked her phone and sure enough, buried in a pile of over a hundred unread text messages were several

24

from Rhea. When she looked at her unopened voicemail messages, she saw the management company's number a half of a dozen times. She was so bent on preparing to get away that she didn't think about anything going wrong. After getting her confirmation two weeks ago, she never thought about it again.

"I'm already here. I really wanted this place."

"I know. I'm truly sorry."

Sorry is what Winter was feeling for herself.

She huffed in sad defeat. She wasn't going to be able to cozy up in front of the fireplace and think back to the last time she'd been here with Dante. She wanted to remember the love. How could she fill her heart and mind with necessary memories if she wasn't in the space where they occurred?

She didn't have a choice. She was here now. She scratched her head in defeat.

"Where is this other place?" she asked.

Winter listened, but didn't really listen as a nervous sounding Rhea provided a rundown of information about the consolation prize house she would instead have to stay in for a month. At least she was in Ridgway. That counted for something.

Her attention was suddenly pulled away from the sound of Rhea's voice at the sound of a car pulling up. The minute she saw the front of the large truck, she knew who it was. Heading her way was the man who'd been on her mind throughout her entire day of travel. It was her ex-husband, Dante. Their eyes locked as if they had each seen a ghost. Perhaps, that's exactly what they were looking at; a ghost of the life they once lived in this very spot. He must be why the house wasn't available.

"Ms. Shaw? Did you hear me?" Rhea asked.

"What was the reason the house isn't available? You mentioned blackout dates. Why this month?" she quickly asked, her eyes not leaving the surprised look on Dante's face. Still, he hadn't exited his truck.

"Oh. Mr. Eastman locked the dates out so that he could stay in the house this month. I didn't realize he had worked this out with another member of the team who only entered it on one calendar but forgot to remove the listing, leaving it open when it shouldn't have been. Again, I'm sorry. Does the house I just described to you work for you?"

Winter's mind drained of everything other than Dante as he exited his truck. Her heart was beating so hard and fast, she was sure he and Rhea could both hear it.

Rhea was still talking in the background, but she couldn't hear her. Her eyes outweighed any thought in her head that she would form to respond. Her mouth was locked with a sudden desire that she hadn't felt in a very long time. That's because the man getting out of the truck was pure Hedonistic perfection.

When Dante closed the door to the truck after taking out his cane, her eyes followed his every single move. Mostly, they focused on this form fitting jeans and rugged black Timberland boots – his staple attire. He was in a short black bomber jacket with his staple men's black with gray Timberland logo knit beanie cap. What she was imagining, but couldn't see were his muscles. Goodness, she missed those muscles. He had on dark sunglasses, but she knew behind them were the most perfect black as coal eyes that had mesmerized her since the first day she'd saw him ten years ago. As he walked in her direction, she noticed an important aspect; he no longer used the cane as a replacement for his wounded leg. Instead, she could see he was less dependent upon it. That was great news.

"Dante?" she said as he walked right up to her on the porch.

"Winter? You're here?"

"Oh, um. Rhea, I'll call you right back," she said into her phone and then disconnected the call.

"You look beautiful," he said.

His compliment surprised her. It came from out of nowhere as if the last time they saw each other they were not the most cordial. It had been at the table where they signed their final papers.

Still, his husky, deep strong voice impressively pulled her in like a moth to a flame. Winter felt like melting into a pool of lust right at his feet. That deep baritone voice and coal black eyes, now that he removed his sunglasses, hurriedly did her in.

"Thank you. I'm sorry for being here. I think there was a mix up. I thought I was renting the house for the month. Your property manager was just on the phone with me trying to explain what happened. I understand that you blacked the days out but they didn't do the proper procedure for doing so."

"You were renting the house? Have you done that before?"

"Oh, no. I wanted a quiet respite to do some writing of a new show I'm hoping to pitch to the studio. While I'm on hiatus from my current show, I thought this would be a great time to get away. I was hoping to do that here. Looks like they found me another house not far from here. I'll get out of your way. You look good, Dante. I see you're walking better."

Winter was nervous. Why? She didn't know.

He didn't respond. Instead, Winter watched his eyes cascade up and down her body. If she was cold at all on this brisk December day, she didn't feel it. She felt nothing but heat. His voice alone, as it always had, was enough to cause that now unknown sexual drive between her legs that she hadn't experienced since him to come alive. She hadn't been ready to spend that kind of time with any other man. She knew that the only face she would see at a moment like that was Dante's.

She happily experienced his eyes and facial expressions when he was aroused, in her mind when she pleasured herself at night, during the day – pretty much every single time she had a need that she never wanted any other man to satisfy. When his eyes gazed at her lips and stayed there, she could barely breathe. Dammit, how could he get her this hot and moist this fast while standing out in the cold?

"I am. I see you're just as gorgeous as ever. Look, let's step inside out of the cold and figure this out," he said walking around her to grab the lockbox.

"No, I don't want to disturb you. I can call Rhea back from my car and get the information on the other house. It's yours for the month."

"Winter? Please come inside out of the cold. It will be dark soon. It's already freezing out here. At least come inside and warmup while this gets worked out. I can get the heat pumping and the fireplaces lit. Please come...inside."

She heard the pause. She even felt it. To her ears, the words sounded enticing. She needed to snap out of the mesmerizing state she was in. She was glad he corrected himself. Between her salacious thoughts every time he spoke, to hearing him say the words, *pumping* and *come* in the same sentence, she could barely keep herself from stripping down to her little, tiny, barely-there thong. Shaking off the carnal thoughts, she nodded and followed him inside.

As Dante moved about turning on lights and upping the heat which was on but not enough to instantly warm them, she let her eyes pan around the large open space upon entry. This area used to be a lot smaller. What she was seeing, she assumed, was a part of the upgrades he made. The large family room was twice the size it had been before.

"Wow – this is amazing. You raised the ceiling and really opened this space up," she happily declared.

"I did. I wanted to provide a view of this area from the upstairs level. There is also a new set of stairs that leads from the upper level to the kitchen. In the past, we could only access the kitchen from the main stairs here in the front of the house. There is an area to overlook the kitchen just like here with the family room. I can't believe you are here. I was thinking about you on the ride here. Isn't that crazy? I was thinking about you and here you are."

They were in each other's thoughts, that's for sure. She wasn't ready to admit that yet.

Winter moved and took a seat on the long sofa in front of the long wall with the fireplace and large television on the wall above it.

"Oh?" she questioned.

"Nothing too crazy. I always think about you when I come here. We had some wonderful times here, especially some holidays when we could get away from work. As I drove close, I remembered we came here after for the last time when we celebrated our Christmas Eve anniversary. That was two years before..."

He didn't finish his sentence. She knew why. He meant to say that it was two years before they divorced. She let it go without drawing too much significance to the month.

"Yes, we did. It's still a lovely place."

"Winter, let's make this easy. Let me help you out with this mix up with the house. I would hate to see you put out due to an error on their end. I'll deal with them after the holiday. I expect better."

"Please don't get Rhea in any trouble behind this issue. She's new. Mistakes happen."

"They do. How about this. If you still want to stay at the house, you can stay here through the end of the month the way you booked it. What do you know about this other house they were able to find for you?"

She didn't know anything. His presence pulling up in his truck distracted her from hearing what Rhea had to tell her about the other house. She wanted to keep things low-key.

"But you're here also. You expected to stay here. Were you staying for the month?"

"That was my plan. Actually, it still is."

Winter sat up straight. Surely, he wasn't about to suggest that they stay in the house together; like old times.

"I see that pretty little head of yours spinning around my words. Don't worry. I'm not planning on staying in the house with you; just on the property. I have my streamer; the trailer that's hooked up to my truck. I stay in it pretty much all year, depending on where in the country I may land. Sometimes I camp outside of it in a tent, but not here. It's way too cold for that."

"I know how much you love camping in the wilderness. Too cold for sure," she replied.

"Correct. That's why I'll stay in my streamer and you can stay here in the house. That is, if I'm not going to disturb your peace if I'm here. I promise to not be any trouble. I'm a pretty quiet neighbor. Now, Pepper is a different story. She can be a little too friendly, though most people love that."

Winter let her eyes dart around the room without turning her head. She was afraid to ask the question swirling between them. He had a woman with him?

She hadn't thought about that. He was with a woman named, Pepper? What type of grown woman had a name like that? She had to know. Before she even asked the question, she was already jealous.

"Pepper? You have a woman with you that you left out in the cold while we've been talking?"

Dante laughed and leaned against the side of the fireplace. He rubbed his hands together as the room slowly heated from the blaze.

"Winter, I would not leave a woman sitting out in the cold either in my truck or in the streamer. Not all of this time. Pepper is my dog. She a French Bulldog with a very playful personality and distinctive bat-like ears. She a beauty with patchy black and white large spots. Trust me, if I'm gone too long from her presence, you would hear her barking for me to let her out. She was fast asleep in the front passenger seat of my truck when I pulled up."

Winter bounced and clapped. She didn't have a dog because of her schedule but she loved them a lot. She really wanted one. French Bulldogs were one of her favorites, coming in a close second to her love for Yorkies.

"Can I meet her? I mean, if you have some time. A puppy? You have to let me meet her."

31

"Of course. She'll be up and looking for me soon. About the house? What do you think?" he asked.

Winter grabbed her bottom lip between her teeth. She really wanted to stay at the house. Putting him out of his own house didn't sit well. Though the elephant in the room, which was any talk about their divorce and time since then, was on the tip of both of their tongues, she assumed, it was clear that now wasn't the time. He wasn't ready and neither was she. Being here for almost thirty days, it would be hard to escape the hardest of conversations. Perhaps, they really could be here together but then, not together.

"Dante, are you sure? I mean, you'll be staying outside of your own house in a, what are they called, trailers?"

"What I have is called an Airstream Classic; technically yes, a trailer. It's literally a home on wheels. It has a separate bedroom, two bathrooms, one is a half which is closer to the front where it slides out to give a lot more space than what is seen when the sides are pulled in. There is a kitchen with a stove, microwave, full-size fridge, two large screen televisions and so much more. I never have a problem sleeping in it for long periods of time. I have a hookup for it on the side of the house. We'll be sharing the water supply but that's it. It has its own power and the truck comes with a power source and its own Wi-fi, so no worries with us having to share that. It's like having two houses on the property. I am as quiet as a mouse. I can't speak for Pepper, especially when she gets feisty."

"Oh, I won't mind Pepper and her barking. You know I love dogs. Never had one because we had crazy schedules. Dogs need attention. I guess you have a lot of time for that since leaving the force."

"I do and I love it. Money is not an issue. I have all the time in the world. The open road is my home wherever I decide to pull over and settle in. This country is beautiful. I'm glad I'm taking the time to take it all in. Take the house, Winter."

"If you really don't mind?"

"Consider it done. Don't even call Rhea back. I gave you the code to the box. I'll give you the code to the door. The same code works on the side and back doors. Besides, if you want or...need...anything, I'll be a stone's throw away. How about I help you get your things into the house and you can meet Pepper?"

Winter stood, nodded and moved toward the door.

"It's something us choosing to be here at the house at the same time, isn't it?"

"You took the words right out of my mouth," Dante acknowledged.

Without words, they stepped back out into the cold. Her only thought was that as soon as he mentioned his mouth, she imagined it all over her; and a sexy mouth he had indeed.

Four

Almost a full week had gone by and Dante was surprised that he hadn't run into Winter even once. After he helped her get her luggage and other bags into the house on that first day, she had played with Pepper while he got his streamer in place and detached from his truck. After that, he had to pull Pepper away from Winter when the hour got dark and it was clear that he and Winter were exhausted. Like him, the day had started early for her as well.

He'd gone out several times during the week. It didn't appear that Winter had gone out at all. The truck she was driving hadn't moved an inch. She did say she was here to relax and get some writing done. He knew how she got when she was focused on a new idea for a show. He'd been her biggest supporter. He even remembered back when she first had the idea for her hit show, *Girl's Trippin'*. It was after she'd gone out of the country on a girl's trip with her friends. They had learned of travel stories from other women while also talking about their own experiences. Winter was the only one of them who was married. She lived vicariously, without jealousy, through them. Out of that came the hit show that people struggled with waiting for the second season. They wanted it now. He wasn't surprised that the studio wanted another hit show from her, hence why she chose the solitude of the house. She'd done that several times at other locations when they were married.

Getting up and moving Pepper off of his lap, he walked over and looked out of the window of the streamer. Winter had the fireplace going inside of the house. He could see the smoke stack at the top of the house. She also had Christmas music playing. This was a time of the year that they both loved. When they were married, they enjoyed the holiday season either with his family or with hers. The fact that neither was doing that with their families this year was some kind of coincidence.

Checking the sky, he looked up to see if it looked like the snow was about to start. He'd checked the weather a few hours ago and about six inches was expected overnight. When he'd gone out earlier, he purposely picked up extra wood for the fireplace just in case Winter needed it. There was already plenty on the front porch and on the back deck. He piled more on so that she wouldn't have to worry about it.

The night before, he had gone into town to first do his laundry before having a few beers with friends he'd met over the years and had stayed in contact with. It was pretty late when he got back to the streamer. After checking the house and seeing that the only light was coming from the family room, he settled in and gathered dinner for him and Pepper.

The moment he stepped inside of the streamer, Pepper was at his feet barking like she was starving. He tried to keep her on a schedule when it came to meals. It was time for her dinner, a little later than usual. Thankfully, he'd left her snack bowl that was timed to provide snacks at intervals that would last until he returned.

In all that he'd done, his thoughts stayed on Winter.

After making himself two large tacos along with some steamed veggies, his favorite side dish, he'd taken a shower, cranked the heat up and he and Pepper relaxed on the leather sofa in the front part of the streamer. Sometime after midnight, he'd turned the lights out, got Pepper's bed together and they were both out for the night.

Tonight, he was going to make two cans of soup and a couple of sandwiches. With snow coming, he was going to catch up on some reading and catch a night time professional football game.

Remembering that he needed to take Pepper out, he slipped on heavy outer gear because the temperature had dropped significantly. He also needed to grab the shovel and other snow preparation items from the storage area in the back of the streamer just in case he needed to shovel snow the next morning.

Getting Pepper's leash, he led her to the door. The pup was already over-excited to be going out. She loved the outdoors as much as he did.

"Let's go for a short walk. Then that's it for the evening until very early in the morning. I'm hoping you won't need to go out again before then. I'll set up your area to go indoors, if you need to."

Pepper barked her agreement before planting her eyes on the closed door. As soon as he opened it and closed it back behind them, Pepper ran around in circles.

They'd been out about ten minutes when the door to the house opened. He turned and looked in that direction.

Winter's sudden presence was now the highlight of his day. Just like on the first day that he arrived, he was thinking of her then and there she was. He was just doing it again.

"Hi, Dante," Winter said, exiting and stepping out on the porch in a sweat suit, large fluffy slippers and a satin scarf around her head. She looked relaxed.

"Hi, Winter. How are you?" he asked and walked closer. It was darker than blue outside. Thankfully, there were lights all around the house to deter unwanted visitors of the animal and human kind. There were even motion sensor lights on all sides of the streamer. They were needed when he was out in the wilderness.

"I'm loving the house. I forgot how much I really love being here. It's so quiet. I don't get that much quiet living in Los Angeles. I'm sure you remember that. It's rather noisy all the time."

"I do. It's one of the reasons I love traveling the country. I find the quietest spots to camp. Is everything working okay in the house?"

"It is. I also noticed the extra wood. I heard you when you put it out. Thanks for doing that. Snow is on the way. I'm all ready to be locked in. Another reason to love being here. The snow-covered mountains are an elegant lady to see."

"I would say it's the prettiest sight, but that would actually be you; even in a silk scarf. You still love those. I love how they look on you. You always look so glamorous. How is that possible around the clock?" he questioned.

Winter tapped her chin and looked up to smile.

"I don't know. I guess I get it from my momma!" she cheered.

"How is your mother? And your family?"

"They're great. I'm getting attitude from them for not coming home for the holiday. They'll survive. They only want me home so that they can get the latest gossip."

"You do have the best secrets of Hollywood stories."

As soon as Pepper realized Winter was there, Dante struggled with the reins of her leash when she tried to race to get to her.

"Hi, girl! Are you loving the outdoors?" Winter asked stooping down to her level.

Dante released her leash. Pepper ran straight for Winter and begged at her feet to be picked up. Winter, of course, obliged her.

"She really likes you. Most times, she's moody and doesn't have time for people to touch her, let alone pick her up."

"Her little legs will get stuck in the snow if the forecast is correct."

"The snow will be shoveled if so. I have a contract with a company to handle that. I also keep a shovel on hand when I don't want to patiently wait."

"Perhaps a white Christmas? Say, are there any holiday decorations here? If not, I was thinking of going into town to get some."

"There are two trees and a ton of Christmas decorations in the storage area. The same code you have for the house unlocks that storage area right off the kitchen. Would you like some help pulling things out?"

"Really? Are you sure? I don't want to keep you from anything."

"Not at all. Pepper and I were about to eat and watch some television. The boxes should be labeled which will make it easy to get out what you want."

"Are you decorating your streamer?" she asked him as they headed inside of the house. When he tried to take Pepper from Winter, his own pup turned her head and looked up softly at Winter. That was a sign that she was happy being in her arms. He wanted to say that he understood the desire to be in Winter's arms. He let it go and headed for the storage area.

His mind, for the past week had been on her arms, her legs, her face, her hair, her behind, her breasts, that area between her legs that he loved burying his head and his body in. He missed her. He'd been with other women since their divorce. None compared to the perfectly amatory feeling he got when he was with Winter. He knew that was why he couldn't get her off of his mind. Being here with her played havoc on his body. He had no right to desire her the way he still did. He was doing fine not being around her. He guessed it was that out of sight, out of mind thing. Having her in his sight had him wanting to be seductively inside of her. Having her on his mind delivered vivid, wicked desires of a nature that could only be satisfied with her. He was a man in lust and still in love with his ex-wife.

When he looked up, Winter and Pepper were walking around and ahead of him toward the kitchen. His eyes landed on her perfect behind encased in a pair of body-hugging black sweat pants. The were made specifically for her flawless figure. He subconsciously licked his lips and then felt ashamed for his thoughts. He was glad she hadn't seen him.

Reaching the storage area, he shook off his spicy thoughts and focused on why he was here. He opened the door to the large room and spotted the Christmas decorations right near the door.

"I see everything is clearly marked. Do you want both trees, or just one of them? There is a ton of everything you would need for a holly, jolly Christmas."

"Just one, unless you want the other one for your streamer."

"No, Pepper and I have a small one that she can't reach. If she could, she would topple it over. Sometimes, she thinks that plants and small trees in the house have the same reason as a tree outside. I like her better trained for outside use of trees for her to do her business," he laughed.

"That's funny. You and Pepper were about to eat? Would you like to join me? I made some spaghetti. There is enough to share. I don't know what you feed Pepper, but I may have something in the cabinets for her too."

"Sure. I'd like that. Do you have any chicken in the freezer or tuna in a can? She loves both. I can also run to the streamer to grab something for her."

"No worries. I actually have both. I'll work on that while you finish what you're doing. Are you sure you don't need my help? You don't have your cane?"

"I don't need it all the time anymore. Normally, just after I've been driving a long distance. With my long legs bent in the driving position for long periods of time, I sometimes need to use the cane for a few steps after I step out. I'm good today. I got great exercise today."

"It shows," Winter said.

With his back to her, Dante didn't let her know that he heard her. Where she tried to whisper, being an ex-cop for years, he was trained to hear and see everything. He heard her loud and clear. He could listen to her speak and never tire.

Five

It was after eleven in the evening when Winter's cell phone rang. She rushed to pick it up from the table in front of her where she was laid out asleep with the television watching her. The fireplace was on full blast. She was snuggled up under a red fleece blanket on the sofa.

"Hello," she answered without looking to see who was calling. Something told her it was one of her friends. They were the only ones who called her at ungodly hours.

"Chick, what's up!" Josie hollered.

"I knew it. I didn't know which one of you it would be, but I knew it was one of the three."

"It's the favorite one. I was calling to check up on you. We haven't talked since you arrived in Colorado. I know we texted but not an actual conversation. Are you getting lots of rest? Doing a lot of writing?"

Winter sat up and turned so her sock-covered feet were on the floor. She wrapped the blanket tighter around her body. Josie was right. She hadn't talked to any of her close friends since she arrived.

For starters, she struggled with telling them that Dante was here. She didn't want to hear the third degree around why she didn't hightail it out of Colorado the moment she saw him. Why she was running from that conversation, she didn't know. At this point in her life, she was tired of explaining herself to anyone.

"Not a lot of writing but yes, a lot of relaxing and rest. I need that more than I need to write."

"That's good to hear. Are there any hot men in Colorado? I know Denver is a big city that's not too far away. There has to be men in Ridgway too, huh?"

"I'm sure there are. I just wouldn't know. I haven't gone anywhere since I arrived."

"What? You haven't checked out the man-meat yet? You're there for a month. It's time you stopped this celibacy thing and get you some. Maybe Santa will send you some good meat for Christmas."

Winter laughed out loud.

"You are so silly. Santa does not drop sexy men at your feet for Christmas."

"Maybe he will do the dropping under the Christmas tree. Do you have one up in the house? Leave enough space for one of Santa's helpers. He might send one to splay him out for you right under your tree. I'm telling you now, I'm declaring that he'll be better than any holiday snack."

"Josie, you have the wildest imagination! Man-meat planted under my tree. And yes, I have one. It's marvelous."

Her thoughts turned to Dante being what she'd love to find under her tree. After all, he did help her put it up.

"Wait, hold on one second. My mom is calling in. Don't hang up," Josie said.

Winter loved the short reprieve. Her thoughts of Dante wouldn't go away. After he helped take out the Christmas decorations, he actually stayed longer, not just to eat with her but to also help her put some of the decorations up. They talked about a lot of things. Still, they avoided what happened between them. They have yet to have that talk. At first, she was bothered that they could be so casual around each other after all that had taken place. Had he forgotten what he took her through? How he threw her away like yesterday's trash? Should she be this nice to him? Should they be this nice and cordial to each other as if their divorce never happened? She couldn't shake the thought that she had a lot to say that she never got the chance to say before. She wanted and needed to let it out. He was being so nice that she didn't want to ruin the mood of them being in the same space. When he and Pepper finally left to return to the streamer, she felt the loss of the connection. It was an immediate blow to her esteem that she had quickly gotten comfortable with wanting and needing him around. Were her friends, right? Should she have just washed her hands of him completely?

"You still here?" Josie shouted, returning to the call.

"Yes, though it's really late. I was actually sleeping, though not in bed."

"Girl, beds are overrated if there isn't a man in it with you."

"Stop lying. You have no problem not having a man in yours. Remember, I am your friend. I know that books, snacks, extra pillows and laundry you haven't put away live on the other side of your bed. Stop playing with me like I don't know."

"Ugh, you're right. That's why I have no problem entertaining men in other rooms in my house. Don't get it twisted. You know how much I love making my way around the male body. So, how is Dante's house? Still loving it?"

And him, Winter said in her head.

43

"Yeah. It's beautiful. He even helped me put up some decorations."

The pause was deafening. She spoke before she thought. This was one of those times when she wished Davina's words had spoken to her before she spoke up. She was often told that she reacts before thinking. That just happened. The elephant had officially entered the room and the conversation.

"Wait, what? Did you say he? Dante is there? He's at the house with you?"

"Shoot. I didn't mean to say that."

Winter kicked herself. Now she had to explain herself.

"Wait before you go all ballistic on me. He's not here at the house, per se. There was a mix up with the reservation. The management company was supposed to black out this month for Dante to be here himself. They didn't do that and we both showed up."

"So where is he if he's not at the house with you?"

"He's staying in his streamer. It's the fifth wheel trailer that he has hitched up to his truck. He offered to let me stay here in the house since I was already here. That was nice of him."

"Nice of him? Girl! That man filed for divorce and left you with the only explanation being that he didn't want to be married anymore. After all you did for him. The way you stood by him after he got hurt and almost died of septic shock from the infection he got in the leg he could have lost if it wasn't for his doctor friend who's a surgeon. He doesn't deserve the right to be kind to you."

"Josie, don't start with me. I don't want to hear it. You, Davina and Tachina have been singing this song for years. Don't call to chastise me like you often do. I'm not a child."

"You're being nice to the man who kicked you to the curb. You think that's okay but you want to get mad at me for checking you on letting him off the hook?"

Winter was getting angry. She hopped up from the sofa and aimlessly walked around the room. She had to walk it off before her angst got the best of her.

"I didn't let anyone off the hook. I was married to him. It ended. We went our separate ways. We are both here after years of no real contact. I'm not going to be ignorant toward him."

"Well, why the hell not? After how he treated you?"

"He was going through a major medical crisis. It was life or death. He lost his career which meant everything to him. He still has bullet fragments lodged in his leg. The fire burned his leg so bad that they had to do a skin graft from skin on his back. All of that did something to him mentally."

"And what about you?"

Winter was losing her patience. She and her friends have been having this kind of conversation for the past two years. Even if she wanted to move beyond the hurt, they wouldn't let her. She had three single friends attacking their only friend who was married. They will never understand. She was over trying to make them.

"Josie, it's late and I don't feel like this tonight. If you and the girls can't let go of this anger around Dante leaving me and allow me to let it go, I don't have anything to talk to any of you about right now. I wanted a month of peace. That includes peace from the three of you stealing my joy. Not this holiday season. I'll talk to later."

Winter did something she's never done before. She ended the call and then turned her phone off. She worked to shake off her anger before turning off the fireplace and the lights. She was ready for bed.

On her way up the steps, she looked out of the large glass window at the streamer. Dante must have gone right to sleep. His trailer was completely dark. The lights on the outside of the trailer were also off. She hated that she couldn't even share with her friend that she enjoyed a peaceful moment between her and Dante. They wanted her to hate him. In her heart, she didn't want that at all. They tried to push her into the arms of other men so that she could replace Dante in her heart. She wasn't sure she ever could. Josie's wish for her for Christmas was for Santa to drop a hot, sexy man at her feet. All she wanted for Christmas was...Dante. Perhaps, that's exactly what the man in the red suit had actually done. She was here; Dante was here. Most of all, her desire for him hasn't ceased or even lessened. Was she foolish for still wanting a man who at some point in their marriage stopped loving her?

She made her way upstairs and climbed into bed. The coldness she felt wasn't about the temperature of the room. It was the emptiness in the space next to her; all around her. It wasn't about any man. Her thoughts were only about Dante as she slipped into slumber.

Six

Dante waited until the last minute to decide that he was going to go out for the evening. The idea of getting fresh air and mingling was exactly what he needed. His potent craving for Winter was consuming him. Thoughts of her were making life in his trailer seem claustrophobic. If he didn't step away from the house with Winter inside of it alone and looking like the gift he wanted to see most under his Christmas tree, he would be ready for a strait jacket. Winter, wrapped in a red bow and nothing else is his ultimate dream and wish for Christmas.

He loved every moment he could set his eyes on her. Each view was more amazing than the last. When she offered him dinner and wanted his help taking out the Christmas decorations, everything in him said that he shouldn't. The plan was not to situate himself back into her life only to end up hurt because his desire was greater than his common sense. What woman would want him after the way he had treated her; her meaning, Winter?

Every time he thought back over that time in his marriage when his words spoke of not wanting to be with her anymore, he knew that was actually the furthest from what he wanted. Something in him refused to let his mouth speak the truth that he wasn't sure he could live without her. He wanted so much for her. Him being permanently injured and scarred wasn't it.

Today, he and Pepper hung out in the trailer while he did his weekly cleanup routine. He was already planning to get out later in the evening when he got a call from a friend he'd met a few years back, Cameron Lymon. He remembered being asked to give an interview to a station in Denver during one of his holiday stays at the house. He had to fly into Denver to do it. That is where, after the interview, he was able to meet Cameron who was one of the most well-known news anchors in this part of the country.

Besides that, Cameron also happened to be the brother of one of the world's biggest action movie stars, Cade Weston. Once he and Cameron had become good friends, his circle expanded to include some of the most elite actors and actresses in Hollywood. He was already part of the inner circle because of Winter's connections.

Cameron had reached out hours ago to let him know that he and his wife, Dakota, were in town at their holiday house with their two kids. After Cameron experienced time away from Denver and checked out the house that he and Winter owned, he decided to purchase a getaway haven of his own without having to go too far from where they lived in Denver. He asked if they could connect. Dakota wanted a quiet night getting the kids settled in. Cameron wanted to take their first night in Ridgway to hang before he buckled down with his family with no interruptions.

After getting Pepper settled with her snack and water bowls until he returned, he put on black denim jeans, black leather boots and a black wool and leather sweater. Grabbing his black bomber jacket, he hopped in his truck to meet up with Cameron.

Dante was surprised when he exited his trailer to see that Winter's truck was gone. She must have finally decided to get out and explore their old stomping grounds. He assumed she was growing a little tired of staying indoors day and night. Other than a few hellos and times when he checked on her to be sure she still had enough supplies, they hadn't spent much time together. She did come out of her house a few times when she saw him outside with Pepper.

One afternoon when he was going out for a bit, she asked if Pepper could hang with her instead of leaving her in the trailer. He agreed. The minute the door to the trailer opened and Pepper raced out, she ran right to the house and inside as soon as Winter opened the door. He shook his head at Pepper not even looking back to give him a look that said, see you later. By the time he got back, he found his pup curled up next to Winter on the floor in front of the television.

As soon as he got to the local hangout spot, which was bigger and better than any big city restaurant, nightclub and pub all made into one, he spotted Cameron inside at a table against the wall across from one of the three bars. From where they sat, with their backs against the wall, something he told all of his friends to do, they could see everything happening inside. There were roughly eight or so tables between them and the bar. Theirs was in a darkened corner.

They had been talking for about thirty minutes, catching up on all of the things they each had been doing since they last connected back in early summer, when Cameron tapped the table and steered his view in the direction of the bar. Sitting at it was Winter. Even with her back to them, Dante was instantly aroused. That seemed to be the state he found himself in at the mere thought of her.

"Winter is here? Are the two of you together?" Cameron asked.

Dante shook his head no. Without taking his eyes off of Winter, he relayed to Cameron how he and Winter ended up in town and at the house at the same time. When Cameron chuckled after hearing the story, Dante did look in his direction. He needed to question his friend's view of the humor in the situation.

"Something funny?" he questioned.

"Bro. Are you serious, right now? Look, I already know how much you want your wife back. I don't know how many other people you've told that to, but you shared that with me when you were in Denver back in, what was that May?"

"Yeah, it was."

Dante focused his attention back on the woman who was the object of his affection and their conversation.

"You don't find it out of this world crazy with coincidence that out of the twelve months in the year, you both end up here at the same time? That is wild. Tell me there isn't some force in the atmosphere that's cheering for you and Winter to work things out."

"Work things out? I don't think so. I told you the things I said to her. No intelligent woman who can get any man she wants and is as gorgeous as she is will consider taking back a man who... I can't even say it."

"You were going through a medical calamity. It was post-traumatic stress disorder, PTSD. Your doctor confirmed that's what you went through. Winter has to understand that you weren't yourself. The problem is, you were up and out of her life so fast without any attempt to work it out that you didn't have time to think through what life would be like without your wife in it. She's always been the woman for you. There has been a lot of suffering on both your parts. Maybe the day has come where it's time to leave the past in the past. Look at how you're looking at her. Do you need a napkin to catch the slobber coming out of your mouth?"

Dante closed his eyes and let his head drop to his chest.

"I don't know."

"You have to tell her how you really feel, not just now, but how you felt back then. Tell her what led you to make that haphazard decision to walk away from your marriage. Dakota and I have had our issues. What I have learned being married is that thinking before acting is important. Isn't that something you were taught as a S.W.A.T. officer? You're a critical thinker. You're quick on your feet and in your mind. Your body and mind went through a life altering change. It's justifiable. I don't see our waitress. I'm going to go grab us a few more beers," Cameron said and stepped away.

Dante tried to catch him, knowing what he was about to do. It wasn't about any damn beers. He wasn't fast enough. Cameron walked right up to Winter. The bartender had just placed a plate of food in front of her when she turned around and saw him sitting in the corner. He smiled like a kid on Christmas morning. Seconds later, Winter was standing at his table with a drink in her hand and her plate in Cameron's hand. He stood and pulled out a chair for her to sit while Cameron raced back over to the bar to grab the beers he lied and said he was getting.

"Taking a break from all that writing and relaxing?" he asked Winter as soon as she was seated.

"Well, I went into town to do some shopping. I wanted

another pair of snow boots and some thicker gloves. I picked up a few other things. I tried to figure out what I wanted for dinner and I remembered this place has the best fried catfish, fried potatoes and onions and best of all, grilled Brussel sprouts with bacon. I didn't feel like cooking, so I decided to stop here. I would say I'm surprised to see you here, but then again, Cameron is in town. I get it."

"Did I hear my name?" Cameron asked, sitting down.

"You did. How is Dakota? I bet the kids are getting big," Winter said.

"She's great. She dragged me out of Denver by my ears. That's usually her signal for when she needs family time away from the big city. I'm always up for that when the time is right. It's good to see you. It's been a long time."

Dante didn't miss Winter's eyes darting to him before turning back to Cameron.

"Yes, it has."

"Well, as much as I would like to catch up, the wife is looking for me," Cameron said tapping the phone in his pocket.

Dante gave Cameron a questionable look after his lame excuse for bringing her to their table and now suddenly, he has to leave. He hadn't been there for more than thirty minutes for an evening where they were planning to play pool in the large room in the back.

"Oh, wow. Are you sure you can't stay?" Dante said, faking his response at Cameron's obvious play for leaving them alone.

He laughed when he noticed Winter had picked up on the ploy as well. He winked at her as they chuckled together.

Cameron stood.

"Look, I'm here for the next couple of weeks. We're spending Christmas at Cade's compound, what I call it, in Florida. I have to get back to Denver to be on the air for the New Year's Eve celebration broadcast. If we can connect again before I leave, let's try and do that."

"Later, man. Tell Dakota hello," Dante said.

"And from me as well. Tell her I'll try and stop by the house one day while you're here."

"How long are you here?" Cameron asked her.

Dante listened while his eyes were focused on Winters lavender colored lip gloss. He felt shameful, but turned-on. He wanted nothing more to taste the flavor of it. He would love to lick it all off.

He thought getting out and away from the house would cool off his spicy wanton lust for her. Having her this close, looking this fine in a pair of snug jeans and a red top that accentuated her gorgeous breasts, he was well overdue for female companionship; but only with Winter. No one else will do.

With her long hair pulled up into a ponytail on the top of her head with long tendrils hanging down, his eyes focused on the small tattoo just below her ear. He wasn't shocked to see that it was still there. It was his initials, DCE in fancy script with a red bow and white arrow in the middle of them. Seeing it ramped up his deepening ache to lean over and kiss her in that very spot. He wanted to remind them both that there was a time when he would get home late from work, slide into bed next to her and place a soft kiss on his initials to let her know he was home. Sometimes she would wake up. Other times, if she was really tired, she would tell him in the morning that she felt his presence when he got it because of his kiss.

"Dante? Did you hear me?" Cameron asked, bringing his mine back to the present after his quick trip down memory lane.

"What? Oh. No. What did you say?" he asked, sitting up straight and clearing his throat in hopes it would clear his steamy thoughts.

"I said, I'm paying the bill on my way out. Later?"

"Oh, sure. Later. Thanks for the invite out though you didn't last long."

"Next time?" Cameron asked on his way out, flashing the peace sign until he reached the door.

"Is Pepper good?" Winter asked, drawing his full attention in her direction.

"She is. I picked up a few extra treats for her yesterday. She's been hiding them and then finding them all over the trailer. I'm sure I'll get back and she'll be in the window in her warming seat. She loves sitting there when I'm driving. The front window is always covered as to keep the heat from the sun and the cold out at night. Are you loving the decorations?"

"I am. Thanks for your help with that. We haven't said much since that night. I understand that we're getting much more snow in two days. Are you ready for that?"

"I am. Snow has become my passion. Now that my leg doesn't work against me in the cold, I can again enjoy the snow."

"Are you sure the trailer is going to be warm enough? I know there are people who live in them all year and in the coldest parts of the country. I have always imagined it to be nights of freezing cold when there is snow like what happens in Colorado."

"It's not cold at all. It's quite toasty inside. You'll have to come over to it one day and tour the entire inside. There are just as many luxuries inside as a house has. There are also many options for keeping it warm in the winter and cool in the summer months."

"Is that a real invitation or was that just something to say?" she asked.

"It is a genuine invitation to you for whatever. When you're ready, you know where to find me."

Before he could say another word, an old school song came on that used to be one of their favorites. Winter stopped eating the moment she heard the smooth sound of the Luther Vandross ballad.

When she looked up at him, he was a goner. He had to be experiencing the same déjà vu moment.

"Dante..."

"Would you like to dance?" he asked, interrupting anything she was about to say.

He watched the lump that formed in her throat. She nodded her answer. He knew why. He was feeling the nostalgia of the moment. He was remembering the many nights they'd made love to the song that had played at their wedding reception.

He got up and took her by the hand, leading them to the middle of the dance floor. They joined a dozen or so other couples.

The minute his arms went down around her hips, pulling her flush against his body, he relished in the feel of her hands sliding up his chest to gather at his shoulders. This is what he's missed. All of Winter; he missed *all* of her. It was this time of year when they got married. The month of December still held a special place in his heart anytime he thought of her. When she looked into his eyes when the song started, he knew.

They swayed together to the sultry, romantic and soulful lyrics.

Winter moved closer to him. He took a chance and gripped her hips tighter. There was no way he could hide his desire for her. It was present between them the way it always has been.

The intense air around them grew possessive and sexy.

"I wanna love, wanna have, wanna hold you girl, so make me a believer."

The song had the impact it always had. Winter held tighter to his shoulders, placing her head on his chest. She moved her hips in sync with his. When she lasciviously held to her, pressing against him so that they could become one, he leaned down, into the area between her shoulder and her neck and whispered.

"Beautiful."

Winter leaned back and looked up into his eyes. She released a heavy sigh. He saw something. Did he see what he thought he saw in her eyes? Was he looking at a returned response of want and longing in her gaze? Could she really want him as much as he wanted her?

He didn't get the chance to ask. Without warning, Winter stepped back from him. No words were shared as she left the dance floor, grabbed her coat and purse and raced to the front door. Just like that, she was gone. He didn't blame her. They were vulnerable. It was clear she didn't want to be. He didn't want to hurt her or have her running away from him because of a moment that may have turned into something that was too much for her. He was ready for her. She was remembering, not the good, but the bad.

Exhaling his defeat, he left the dance floor and returned to the table. He didn't leave. He sat and thought about the loving moment they just had; the first in over two years. Back then, it was okay because they were husband and wife. Now? Not so much. He'd left her at a time when their love hadn't dissipated. His feelings of being the man she married and deserved had. What could he do now? What could he say? How could he get her to believe that he never stopped loving her.

Deciding to stay and listen to the music was all he could do. Winter needed her space. It couldn't be forever. They needed to talk. Cameron was right. There was so much that was left unsaid that needed to be said. For now, he would let it go.

Seven

Three hours.

Winter checked the time on her cell phone again. Three hours after she left Dante standing in the middle of the dance floor, he had finally arrived back at his trailer. She had tried several times to get to sleep, but it eluded her. Tossing and turning from one side of the bed to the other was all she was able to achieve. Her mind wouldn't turn off. It wouldn't let her loose from the image of her in his arms ready to scream that she still loved and wanted him. She could feel how much he was aroused dancing with her. That song always did that to him; and to her. His body left no doubt of that. Neither did hers. Though not as visible as that part of him that was long, thick and pressing strong against her stomach, she could take off her thong and her essence would drip all over the floor.

On the dance floor, she knew what had done her in. It was hearing him hum the words; whispering to her that she was beautiful. She couldn't take anymore.

Dante was and has always been her superman. That was why she fell in love with the song. Until she'd met him, it was just a song from an artist she loved. The song was magical now. So was her love for Dante. It had never gone away. She was still stuck back in time when they loved each other conditionally; until he no longer did. That's what sent her running away from him. He was her wonderland.

    She smiled to herself thinking about the day she first called him her winter wonderland. He was initially confused not understanding what the words meant. She then explained that whenever they made love, he had no boundaries to letting her get from him and his body everything she needed. Until him, she'd never experienced performing oral sex on a man. With Dante, it was easy. He never brought up the fact that she'd never loved him that way, though he was never shy about loving every part of her with every part of him. Shyly, she'd asked him to show her how to please him that way.

    Dante had been patient with her when he went through what it was that men loved about oral sex. She absolutely loved when he did it to her. Once she knew what he loved, it became one of her favorite ways to love on him. She enjoyed it as much as he did. After that first time, she loved that his body belonged to her. She could touch, caress, kiss, lick, taste and love on him in any way she chose. She loved exploring his body and the way he responded to her. Those were the thoughts she experienced tonight seeing him. She wanted to explore her wonderland again. Her wonderland was his body. There was never a time that she wasn't hot for him; including right now. Surviving the rest of the month without his kiss or his touch was sure to drive her mad with unadulterated lustful thoughts. Her need for him was that pure. The places on him that her mouth and her tongue enjoyed loving were only a few steps away from her doorstep.

    The time on her phone read one in the morning. The house was completely dark. She didn't even bother to turn a light on once she arrived at the house. After parking the truck, she raced inside and right up the stairs. Before she could do anything else, she raced to the shower, ripping her clothes off as fast as she could. Turning the water on its coldest setting she stepped under the stream in hopes that the cold water would cool her overheated body, namely the area between her legs. Her body was on fire in a way that she hadn't experienced in a long time. With one hand on the wall, she had moved the other between her legs. She had a sure-fire way to give herself the relief she felt vital to her very existence.

Before getting too far along, she removed her hand and placed them both on the wall of the shower in front of her. When the water got too cold, though her body hadn't calmed any, she changed the setting to hot and showered. The shower did give her a little relief. She was able to cry in peace and her tears were washed away along with the soapy suds that streamed down her body. Not seeing herself crying helped her forget that she actually had. She cried through how pathetic she felt still loving Dante. The past still happened. Her bare wedding ring finger was a constant reminder.

After putting on her two-piece, white, fleece pajama set, she climbed into bed and prayed that sleep would come fast. For about thirty minutes, it had. Then she grew curious as to whether Dante had left shortly after she had left the bar. After looking out of the window to where his truck would have been parked, the spot was empty; so were her hopes that he was concerned about the reason behind her hasty exit. Did he even care? Was she expecting too much?

Getting back in the bed, she tried to find sleep again. She found herself drifting in and out but nothing steady. She had only nodded off into a light sleep. That's how she was able to hear his truck pull up almost an hour ago. Like her, he didn't appear to turn on any lights inside of the trailer. He did take

Pepper out to do her business. That didn't last long as he usually did; allowing her to run around to burn off energy. This time, as soon as Pepper was done, he picked her up and went back inside.

Standing at the window for about fifteen minutes, she waited for any sign that he was up thinking about her like she was thinking about him. He had to be. She couldn't be on this wild ride by her lonesome. Dante had to be as confused as she was about how they had reached this place. She wanted him. She knew that. He wanted her. She felt that. Was the desire strictly physical? Sexual? Was there any part of his heart that still yearned for her as hers did for him?

Hopping back in bed for the third time, she crawled back under the thick blankets, snuggled with the pillows until she was in the perfect position for sleeping and waited for slumber to greet her. Another thirty minutes, and nothing. The only thing she found was how wonderfully quiet the room was. Suddenly finding it an uncomfortable quiet, she reached for her phone and played some soft music. Then she felt too warm under the three blankets. She usually loved the heavy blanket feeling. Tonight, not so much.

"Ugh! What is wrong with me?" she yelled into the darkness.

Realizing sleep wasn't happening, she slid her body from her cocoon and placed her feet on the floor. Her eyes landed on the window that overlooked outside. She walked slowly over to it again. Her thoughts were wild. Was Dante sleeping soundly? Had he already forgotten how sensual things had turned on the dance floor? The moment had gone from zero to sixty fast.

Did Dante believe that they were only dancing? Was he

like her and assumed that the dance was a prelude to something else which was her reason for acting like the runaway bride? If he was sleeping, she was even madder. She couldn't sleep, why should he?

"That's it!" she bellowed.

Grabbing her thick, pink fleece robe, she headed for the stairs. She needed to talk to him. No way was she going to get a good night's sleep until she spoke her mind. Was it his intention to get her all hot and bothered? He had to know what that song would do to her. He didn't have to ask her to dance.

Finding her pink boots near the door, she slipped into them, turned the alarm off on the house and opened the door, pulling it tight behind her. Instead of her key, she keyed in the lock code and waited until she heard the click that the door was secure.

It was now or never. Deciding on now, she headed for the trailer. Gathering up all of her nerve, she first knocked on the door and then pushed the small doorbell to the left. He had to know she was there. All of the lights around the top of the trailer came on. She listened for any movement. Hearing none, not even Pepper, she was hit with a wave of doubt. This impromptu visit to his trailer was not a good idea. She started to turn around when the inside door opened. Standing shirtless on the other side was Dante looking like the Adonis version of him she often dreamed of. No man should be this fine.

Why? Why did he have to open the door without a shirt on?

"Winter?" he asked looking around. "Are you okay?"

"Um, can I come in?"

"Of course. First tell me that you're okay? Did something happen?"

"No. I'm sorry if my showing up made you worry. I'm okay. I just want to talk."

"Really? At this hour? Okay. I'm game if you are. Come on in. It's freezing out there."

Insider, her eyes widened the moment the lights came on. Her eyes landed on what looked like a luxury apartment. She had no idea trailers were this big.

"You said it was large inside, but this is incredible. I see why you have no problem living in it full-time."

"It has all of the pleasantries of a home without all of the maintenance. You wanted to talk?" he asked.

Winter tried to rush her mind to organize her thoughts. Seeing him without a shirt was a distraction. She needed to refocus.

"Where's Pepper?" she asked.

"In her bed next to my bed in the back. I'm surprised she's not up. Usually when the lights come on, she's up being nosey."

"Like a typical woman, huh?" she joked or tried to.

The smile on Dante's face said that he got the meaning.

"I guess so. Can I get you something? I know it's the middle of the night but we're both up."

"No. I just want to talk."

"Okay."

Winter gathered her courage and went for it.

"What was tonight?"

Dante hunched his shoulders.

"I think I'm going to need a little more information."

"The dance. The song. The…"

She paused. There was no way that he couldn't know what she was talking about.

"I wanted to dance with you," he said.

"Dante, don't do that. I know you know what I'm talking about. Something is going on and I'm confused. It's been two years since we've even seen each other. Somehow, this time that we've been here so far is as comfortable as we were when we were married. Except, we are staying in two different houses."

"We've connected."

"But that's it, Dante. We aren't supposed to connect. You *left* me!" she shouted.

The words came out louder and harder than she had planned. She spoke what was on her mind.

When Dante clasped his hands together and leaned against the square table in the middle of sectional leather table seating, she waited. He closed his eyes before opening them and focusing on her.

"Okay, Winter. You came here to talk, so let's talk. Tonight isn't something I'm going to apologize for. Even before the song, I've wanted you. There, I said it. I know you felt it."

"I felt it. But, why? You left me. You didn't want me. Now you're being nice and cordial. I'm felt...you. You're making me feel good and mushy. I've been imagining us and I shouldn't be. Why? Because you threw me away. Remember that? Why am I getting a vibe that you're trying to say something but not saying it at the same time? What are you doing to me? Please don't play with me. I can't handle it. I'm already struggling with being here with you. Unlike you, I have not been able to turn my emotions on and off to suit the moment."

"What's wrong with me wanting you? I can't turn that off.

Since I've been here, all I have done is want you."

"What about before now? Were you hating me? Were you happy to have your freedom? I thought what you wanted was to be away from me. I get it. We're here by happenstance. That doesn't mean what it used to mean."

"I get that. I'm sorry if I made you uncomfortable with the dance."

"Why?" she asked.

He looked mystified.

"Why what?"

"I didn't get closure. Signing divorce papers and walking away wasn't closure for me. I loved you. With everything in me, I loved you. I did what I thought a wife was supposed to do, especially after you got hurt. I was there around the clock. I did what you wanted and needed. Still, it wasn't enough. You tossed me away. You made me feel like I wasn't worthy to be your wife anymore. No matter what I did, you shouted at me. You preferred everyone else helping you but me. Then one day you told me that you'd had enough and you wanted out. For months, I tried to understand that. I couldn't. I never have. It seemed like just as easily as we married, it all came to an end. I still don't know why. You fought for everything but me. You fought to get better. You fought to find your place in life. But me? You left me feeling like I was less than."

"Baby, I am so sorry."

Dante moved in her direction and tried to take her hands. She took a step back out of his reach.

Before she could stop, she cried. First it was an easy cry. Then the memories of the feelings she went through and cried herself to sleep about for months hit her. The dam broke and she cried so loud and hard that she woke Pepper up. The puppy raced over to her as she continued wailing as if she was in physical pain. Dante again reached for her but she held her arm out to hold him off.

"Don't. You have no idea what I went through. You left me to rebuild my life like I hadn't been married to the man I thought I would spend the rest of my life with. How could you do that to me like that? *How!*" she cried.

Dante reached for and handed her some tissues. He then did move in her direction in order to help her sit down. She wiped her eyes and her nose. The tears wouldn't stop. He knelt down in front of her.

"Listen, I mean it when I say I'm sorry. I could blame it all on what I went through and PTSD that I was diagnosed with and possible bipolar disorder. I can't explain what was going on in my head. I've spent two years in therapy. I've learned a lot about myself that I should have stuck around in our marriage and gone through with you. My two years have been lonely. They've been hard because I've missed you. What I can say is that I did not want to hurt you. I know I did and I can't take that back. It happened and will always be in the atmosphere and the space between us. I get that. Can I explain my feelings from then to you now? Can you give me time to do that?" he pleaded. "Please, Winter," he begged.

She looked into his eyes and knew that she wouldn't be able to deny him anything. She came here tonight to get her closure. She could only get that if she allowed him to share. Even if his words hurt or cut her even deeper, she needed this. There was still a part of her that was hurting like it was the day he walked out on her.

She took a moment to decide if she wanted to hear his truth. She was here. Yes, the time was now.

"The floor is yours," she said through tears and huffing as her body slowly calmed from her intense crying.

She sat back in the chair while Dante stood and leaned back on the table. Facing her, she prepared her mind and her heart for what he was about to share. It's what she asked for. He was about to give it to her.

Eight

"Winter, there is something about back then that you don't know. That day before I left, I was at my doctor appointment with Zane. I had a breakdown while I was there. I flipped out hearing that I would never be able to be a S.W.A.T officer again. I can walk better now because I had my knee rebuilt after we separated. A few bullet fragments still remain, but the leg is so much better."

"What!" she yelled.

"I'm sorry you're finding out like this."

"No one told me. Your mother, Zane, no one. How could they keep that from me?" she questioned.

He heard her pain. He needed to continue.

"We were separated and heading for divorce. Nothing was contested so we didn't have to see each other. I demanded their secrecy. I didn't think that after we separated, that I shouldn't be a burden on you anymore. That breakdown broke me to pieces. I promise you, my leaving had nothing to do with who you were as a woman or as my wife. It was all me. I didn't feel like I was ever going to again be the man you married. I had a limp. My body was scarred from the fire. My knee was shattered. I had Zane take me to appointments so that I could hide from you how serious my injuries were. I didn't want you to see me as an invalid. I felt lesser than the man you deserved. I didn't want you to be stuck with me."

"Did you even know me? You didn't know that I would have been there because we would have had each other? That's all that was important."

"I know that now. I didn't know that then. I was angry at the world. I was angry at myself for going into that building. I almost lost two of my team members. In trying to save them, I got shot twice in my knee. That damage was devastating. When I heard those two kids in that house screaming when that thug tried to burn the house down around them, I had to act. I had to get to them. I crawled to them, shattered knee and all. That's when the beam that was already on fire fell on me. The heat was so intense that by the time they reached me, even my clothes had burned into my leg. I was a mess. I wasn't Dante Eastman anymore. I wasn't S.W.A.T. team lead Dante anymore. I didn't know who I was. What I knew was that I wanted to get away from everyone and wallow in self-pity. My biggest mistake was taking it out on our marriage; on you. I've been sorry ever since. I have never, ever stopped loving you. I never stopped wanting you. I have never stopped desiring you. That didn't happen just by being here with you. It's always been there. I had too much pride to go back after all that I had said and after the divorce to tell you that I had made a bid mistake."

"That time was hard for us both, Dante. You weren't in that alone. I wanted to fight for us. I tried to do that."

"I know. I don't know the man I became. I can't take it back. I wish I could, but I can't. I was horrible to you. I'm sorry. The dance tonight was the first time that I've held you that close in a long time. I didn't want to let you go. I wanted that song to play all night long. I've yearned for you for a very long time. I couldn't believe I was holding you."

"I was so hurt. I was damaged, Dante. Mentally and emotionally, I struggled some days to even get out of bed. I thought loving you would be enough for you to know that damaged knee, burned parts of your body, no longer being that officer – none of that mattered to me. It never did. I can't believe you didn't trust me enough to love you through anything."

"I didn't want you to have to take care of me. You didn't sign up to take care of half a man."

"Don't say that. Don't you *ever* say that! I signed up to always be with you no matter what. You weren't nor will you ever be half of a man. You took away my choice to love you through all of what you were going through. I was willing to still choose you. You didn't choose me. What am I supposed to do with that?"

Dante wasn't sure he was telling her enough to justify acting like none of that ever happened. That's what he did tonight when he held her in his arms. He acted as if everything that led up to their divorce had never happened.

"Can I choose you now? I know I don't deserve you now like I deserved you back then. A lot has happened. It's not about being lonely or even trying to make up for time that we can never get back. I'm a different, better person now. I understand myself better. I know that my career or even having a perfect leg isn't who I am. I've been driving around this country missing you like crazy. I haven't been able to find myself because a part of me was still with you. I don't deserve to ask you for anything. I know that. I'm telling you that I made a horrible, horrible mistake. So much has happened. I know I hurt you. If I could take that pain from you and bring it on me, I would do that."

Winter couldn't believe her ears. He wanted them again.

"Trust me, you wouldn't want anything to do with how I felt. It was bad."

"I'm sorry."

If he had to repeat those words forever, he would do it. There had to be a way to give them a second chance.

"I was restless tonight. I couldn't sleep. I left that bar because I needed to breathe. In that moment, I would have forgiven any and everything you made me feel. I desired you. I needed you. I wanted you. Then I felt like I was forgiving you too easily. It shouldn't be as easy as you saying you're sorry and me considering anything other than taking that apology and finally going on with my life. I came here to absolve myself of the guilt of feeling like I wasn't enough. You did that to me."

Before he could respond, Winter got up and turned toward the door. He knew he had to do something. Letting her leave like this can't happen. He did this to her once. Though she had every right to walk out on him, something told him that it wasn't what she wanted just as much as it wasn't what he wanted.

Moving with a quickness, he stumbled over Pepper who was prepared to follow Winter out of the door. He walked up close to her and wrapped his arms around her waist from behind. He could feel her body shaking as she again cried. He felt tears in his own eyes starting to form. Unless there was no way in hell that she would ever take him back, even just to date to see how it would go, he wasn't going to give up.

"I love you, Winter. I always have. I know you don't want to hear those words. At one time, they meant the world to us both. I really, truly love you. I never stopped. I was just too stubborn to tell you, to come for you, to fight for you. I should have. We have no business being in this position of living two separate lives. I have money. I have freedom. I have the open road. I have everything that I feel I need except for you. You are what is missing in my life. Can you try to forgive me? If not, can you give it a start even if your forgiveness takes years? I don't want to be without you again."

Winter smelled wonderfully. She smelled like lavender and peach. That was her favorite scent. Because it was, it was his too. She didn't move or say a word. She stood in his arms. He wasn't being pushed away. This was a start.

He caressed her arms and leaned his head down to her shoulder. He saw the tattoo.

"Dante..."

"Don't say no. Please, Winter. I promise, if you give me a chance, I can show you that I'm a changed man. Therapy has helped me come a very long way. I have appreciated how it has helped me grow. I have been working on the man I am hoping you would want again. I would do anything. I love you," he repeated and then did what he's been dreaming of doing. He kissed his initials.

Outside of the trailer, he could hear the wind picking up. They were expecting some snow in the next few hours. He would love nothing more than to fall asleep with her in his arms. It would be asking a lot. He was about to plead even more when she stepped out of his embrace. He dropped his shoulders when he thought all he'd said had fallen on deaf ears. He expected her to keep on walking to the door. Instead, she turned around and faced him. Tears were still running down her cheeks. He wiped every single one of them away. He leaned forward and kissed her cheeks where the tears had been.

"You really hurt me," she uttered softly.

"I love you, Winter. Can you at least believe that I mean that?"

He used his finger to raise her head to see her eyes. They were full of tears. She didn't look away.

"I don't know if I can go back. No matter what my body may crave, I don't think my heart can go through being let down by you again. I hear your words."

"This month. The time that we're here," he said.

"What about it?"

"I'm here. You're here. We were married. I know your body. You know mine. Do you remember how we used to make love all over that house? Not that it wasn't hot and sexy everywhere, but especially here on those cold winter days and nights. The passion between us is unmatched. It may not be right, but I can't stop thinking about those times. Quenching our zestful thirst for each other. The way you feel gripping and holding me inside of you. The kind of erotic satisfaction that we found the moment I entered your body. I don't know about you but I've been in a constant state of arousal since I laid eyes on you back on the first. Yes, I broke up our marriage. I will live with that for the rest of my life. For the rest of the month, let's lean into our carnal desires for each other. If you don't feel the same way when you're around me? Okay. Would you like to try and deny that you're feeling what I'm feeling? I absolutely dare you to. Before you do, I should remind you that I can see and smell when you're in need. Pheromones.

Your scent attracts me like a snake charmer does a snake. That may not be the best description, but I know you understand. Do you want to declare that I'm wrong about what I would find if my head was pressed between your legs? No doubt that you can feel me."

With his hands caressing her shoulders and then down her arms through her robe, he felt it. He knew what was happening.

"I can't," she whispered out.

"You're shivering," he shared.

"I can't help it. It's what you do to me and you know it. I want to deny it; I would be lying."

"I've missed you," he whispered close to her ear. "The rest of this month is all I'm asking for. I don't deserve even that – I know. I'm still going to ask. I'll even beg."

Dante smiled to himself. He needed her to be as turned on as he was. By the way she was reacting to his touch, she was.

"I've missed you too."

"Enough to allow me to love on you for the rest of this month? Anytime, anywhere and anyway that you want. Do you know what I'm remembering?"

Winter laid her head back against his chest. Her hands fell to her side in surrender.

"No. What?"

He pulled her with him to where he leaned back on the small table. He turned her around in his arms so that she was snug against his body once again.

He heard it. Her sound was faint, but he heard it. Her sexy sigh of knowing sexual relief could be happening tonight was evident to his ears. His keen awareness was always on point; especially when it came to her.

"Your wonderland. You always called me your winter wonderland. You loved playing with my body to your satisfaction."

"You always let me."

Dante smiled again and looked down in the small space between their bodies. She was moving her hips from side to side against his raging hardness. He has never been shy about his reaction to being close to her. He wasn't about to be now.

He reached down to her hips and pulled her behind back against him to the point that he couldn't see a space between them. He let her get what she needed from where they stood.

Moving his hands up from her hips to her sides, he moved them around to the front of her body. Without untying her robe, he moved his hands inside of it and splayed his hands across her breasts.

With his head lowering, he placed open-mouthed kisses across her neck to her shoulders.

"If you agree, I will for the rest of this month. We're here. You know I can satisfy every single one of your needs. No question you do the same for me; you always have."

"Then..."

She didn't say it, but he knew what she was trying to say. He finished for her.

"Then why did I break up our good love? Our good life? I was stupid. That doesn't take away from how good we are together in bed. Would you agree?"

"Yes. Mmm," Winter moaned out when he nipped at her neck. When she stretched her neck to give him better access, he pulled her close while his hips going in a circular motion drove them mad with untamed ardor.

"Then?"

"The month?" she responded.

Unbuttoning her white pajama top, he removed enough of them, allowing his bare hands to reach inside to caress her flesh. From his first touch, her nipples pebbled into hard tips the way he loved. The large, perfectly formed mounds were much more than a handful.

Dante was so nervous about handling her that his hands shook. He turned her around again so that they were facing each other. His eyes dropped to her lips. That's what he needed. It was her lips.

"Is the house locked up?"

She looked up at him, her eyes barely opened. There was a sexual haze to them.

"Yes."

"Good because I doubt if you'll make it back there before daylight. I'm not sure we'll even get any sleep. I've waited too long to have you."

Dante said the words but didn't wait for her to respond. He lowered his head, aligning their mouths for an impending intoxicating joining. Winter's eyes fluttered until they slowly closed and then opened again. He was almost done for when he saw the fire in them just before they dropped and focused on his lips. She had to be wondering what he would do next. He didn't make her wait.

Slipping his lips over hers, he feasted on her, slowly yet deliberately. Nothing about the kissed was rushed. He went painstakingly slow to allow their minds to savor the feel of reconnection on an immeasurable plateau. Winter then took control. Pulling her lips away and her eyes stayed on his, she lowered her lips to his chest. When she moved them to his chin, planting soft kisses there, he was close to losing all of his faculties when her lips caressed, sucked and licked on his neck. That move heightened his desire for her. She knew that it would.

He made quick work of her robe and pajama top, leaving her naked from the waste up.

"I miss this," she whispered against his chest as her lips covered every piece of flesh she could reach.

With Winter busy getting her fill, he moved her pajama bottoms down her hips until she could kick them off. His eyes widened when they landed on her womanhood, free of panties of any kind. He loved her like this while also remembering her body in some of the sexiest thongs of all styles and colors. His favorite color on her was always pink.

Though he reminded her that they had all night, he was in a rush to get a taste of what he'd been denied due to his own foolish choice.

To his eyes, there is no better site than Winter being naked. He had to touch more of her before he passed out like a school boy about to have sex for the first time. He slipped his hands down over her breasts, moving his body down her body. He kissed her stomach and made wet paths across it. Sinking down further, he slipped his hand between her legs, parting them slightly. When his lips found the top of the thin strip of hair that led to that soft, silky part of her, he moved a finger between her legs, caressing her ever so slowly. The excessive moisture he found there told him that she was excited for him before she had even entered the trailer.

Looking up, his eyes captured the moment Winter drew her bottom lip between her teeth to stifle the frenzied, high-pitch scream he knew she wanted to let lose. Her body shook from his caress. Her hands and nails dug into his shoulders.

She threw her head back with tightened lips to smother even more cries he knew she wanted to release into the air around them. He was just as turned on by the sounds of the wetness his fingers slid through over and over, driving her and him wild with all-consuming anticipation.

When he slipped first one, then a second finger inside of her, her pliant body was about to give way to collapsing. He held her to him with his free hand palming her behind.

Dante dipped his head further and replaced his fingers with his lips and tongue, darting it out salaciously across the hard nub that silently screamed his name. He feasted on her like a starving man. He was getting all that he'd been craving. He was giving Winter all that she wanted and needed. Between a sexy sucking motion and flickering his tongue over her most sensitive area that hardened with readiness, he felt the moment Winter gave into the overwhelming, yet electric feelings that seared through her. An immediate orgasm shattered her into a million sexy pieces. He marveled at how alluring she looked in the midst of an orgasmic high. Her body reacting to him was just as much for her as it was for him. Not wasting another moment, he braced himself, still with his head between her legs and stood, supporting her body twirling wildly on his lips. He turned and moved them to the bed.

Placing Winter on her, he placed a finger between her legs to keep the delightful friction going as he removed his sweat pants. Spreading her legs further, he leaned over and kissed her deeply, allowing her own essence to stoke the fiery need for more of what he'd just given her; an all-powerful release.

"A prelude, baby. Just a prelude to the rest of the night," he uttered against her lips.

She moaned because he knew that a reply wasn't necessary. Not only did she know his body as her playground, her wonderland; he knew hers and what would send her flying.

Before she lost the sexual haze that covered them, he parted her legs with his hips, masterfully sliding between them. Knowing how ready for him she was, he knew joining them would be an easy and worthwhile journey.

Entering her slowly, he was surprised at the tightness he found. He slid in a little and then pulled out, lifting his body slightly to gaze into her eyes. She knew what he was going to ask even before he got the chance to do so.

"No one else," she mewed in heated delight. "There's been no one else since you," she added and then pulled him back in for a steamy kiss.

"You are so beautiful, baby. You feel so much like mine; all mine. I'll go slow. Just mine," he murmured against her opened mouth.

His jaw was tight. The feel of Winter's body wrapped so tightly around his rigid, swollen flesh.

"I know what it feels like to you. I need you. I want all of you. Don't hold back," she purred.

"You feel like you've been needing me for a long time; as long as I've been needing you."

Winter moved her hips up and off the bed just as he slid further inside of her. Giving her a little of his engorged hardness at a time was important to him. He wanted her to feel only pleasure with no pain. She writhed sexily beneath him the further he slid into her body. He pulled out until only the tip of his strong erection remained. Pulling her body to the very edge of the bed, he moved forward and gave her all of him. He kissed her deeper, using his tongue to enter her mouth in sync with the rhythm he'd set for entering her body with power strokes.

The sensation of being back inside of her was sensationally wicked. Picking up the rhythm he'd set, he filled her body, harder and deeper beyond what they had ever experienced in the past.

Dante was losing control of his need. His sanity was going out the door as his strokes surged powerfully in and out. Winter encouraged him on with her own rhythmic strokes up, down and around his hardened flesh. The way her body stretched for his entry drove him higher and higher.

Winter's head thrashed about from side to side as an intensive explosion had her losing control. He was right along with her. Her hands gripped him tight; her nails dug into his back as her release gripped her and wouldn't let go. Dante tried to keep his eyes on the beautiful sight before him of the woman he loved as she gave into the shaking quakes that seized every part of her and him.

Sweat poured from his head down to her chest as his body let go while immersed in the sounds of gasps and moans. Winter wrapped her legs tight around his hips, lifting her hips to meet each of his thrusts. The feeling was the last vestige of strength he had left. Winter rocking her body into his sent his body shooting off like a rocket into space.

Explosive currents tore through his body as shivers of delight caused his orgasm to rip through. He pumped fiercely, filling her with harmonic laced, uncontrolled love from a place deep within. He surrendered completely to the love and seduction her body claimed his with. Winter had all of him. She always had; even during their time apart.

As their bodies took their time calming, he was reminded how perfectly they fit together. It wasn't about the powerful sex they'd just had and would have again, it was about reclaiming the connection that never should have been broken.

Winter held him close to her. She helped soothe his still excited body to help him control his ragged breathing. When she tried to wipe the pouring sweat from his head, he leaned up and poured his gratitude for this moment into a tantalizing kiss.

"Are you okay?" he asked, pausing between each word. He was still working to control his breathing.

"Okay? I am better than okay. That was out of this world. Your leg," she noted and then tried to lean up to check him over. They had been so caught up in the moment, so his leg was the last thing he was worried about.

"My leg is fine. It's feeling as good as the rest of me. In fact, I think my leg is ready for more. I'm reveling in the feel of how snug you feel around me."

"I can feel that. I see some things haven't changed."

"When I'm inside of you? There will never be a change. There will always be more."

Moving their bodies further up the bed, he changed their positions, placing her on top.

"Mmm, I see you know that I haven't changed. I love being on top."

"I'm your wonderland, remember? Have at it, baby! We're in this together. This kind of good loving doesn't go away; no matter what or where we are. Who I am has changed. Who you are to me hasn't changed. What we are together is beyond even this."

Winter moved into position and slid down over him. She didn't move like he thought she would. She stilled her body.

"I want to just sit like this for a minute. A month will come and go before we both know it. I don't want to forget anything about right now."

"Take as long as you want. We have all-night."

When Winter began to move, he knew that there was no way he'd be able to let her go after the month was over. All he could do was hope that she would come to feel the same. He grasped her hips and enjoyed the here and now.

**

Winter stretched so long and hard after waking that she felt like she was rising from a long winter's nap. In her stretch, her body ached in places that she forgot could so pleasantly. Each time she moved, she was reminded of the exquisite level of loving Dante had bestowed on her, of course, knowing that she needed it. Only he could touch her and know exactly what part of her needed him the most. Last night, it was all of her.

Thinking she would roll over in Dante's bed and find him, she was surprised when the other side of the bed felt cold and distant. He was gone.

Sitting up, she moved to the foot of the bed and looked down at Pepper's bed and saw that she was also not in the trailer. Before she could lay back down, she saw a note on the wall to her left from him telling her that he took Pepper out for her morning walk, or rather stroll in her puppy stroller. Winter smiled remembering how cute Pepper looks when she refuses to walk even one more step. Dante bought her a stroller that he'd put her in so that he could get through his run with her still in tow. It was cute to see the pup loving being in it and still enjoying being outdoors.

The trailer was completely dark inside except for a few soft lights that led from the bedroom area to the front of the trailer, providing a path to move around without turning lights on. She assumed it was still dark outside until she reached for her phone and saw the time. Her mouth opened with a gasp. It was after nine in the morning. She couldn't remember the last time she'd slept this late. No doubt she was well rested after the marathon kind of night they'd shared.

She thought back to how she got here. They hadn't done a lot of talking after Dante picked her up and carried her to his bed. Her body was screaming at him to take her before she gave herself a heart attack from desiring him at a level she had only experienced in the past with him, and only him.

Laying back in bed, she crossed and uncrossed her legs and loved the feeling that surged deliciously through her body. Oh, if only she could have reached over and encouraged Dante to give her more. She didn't know how long this free-for-all sex-capade would last with him; if at all. Was last night the only night? He asked for the rest of the month. Was that thought shared at the height of his desire for her? Yes, she wanted him. Images of what they could share in a month was a titillating idea. In silence, was she not specific enough when she asked Santa to have him under her tree? Surely, he couldn't have thought that she meant for one night only. Quick disappointment at that idea was quickly dismissed when the door to the trailer opened. The gorgeous hunk of a man that she'd just been thinking about walked in and looked right at her before turning on aa dim light. The night before was in his eyes. Together, they were remembering it all. She craved more of him. Her heart raced and her lady parts came to life at the sight of him.

Pepper saw her and barked until Dante finally put her down. She raced right up to the bed. Winter moved quickly, thankful that she wasn't fully naked but had on one of Dante's shirts. The moment she picked Pepper up the puppy whimpered with delight.

"Good morning," Dante said, now distracting her from the love she was getting from Pepper.

"It's almost afternoon, isn't it? You let me sleep this late? I'm an early person," she joyfully explained.

"Usually is the correct word. Just not for today. None of my moving around got a rise out of you. Pepper needed to go out and I needed to get my morning run in. For some reason, I felt invigorated. I needed to stretch my leg."

"Well, I wonder why."

"I don't wonder. The answer is you," Dante joking replied.

"Come, let me massage your leg," she offered and removed the blanket that covered her body. She wanted him to know, without any doubt, that that massage could lead to anything else he wanted, especially what he could see from where he stood.

She placed Pepper back on the floor. Seconds after finding her comfy spot on her bed, her eyes closed.

Winter was now ready to concentrate on the man in front of her.

"I guess she's exhausted," Winter said.

"I'm thinking you kept her up with all that moaning and howling you were doing."

Winter laughed as heartily as Dante had. Their eyes were quietly sharing that they knew why the night was loud.

"Oh, like your growling didn't wake the animals out in the woods," she replied.

"True, true. How are you feeling this morning? A little sore?"

Bashful, she turned her eyes away and nodded her head. Winter wondered if he had noticed how she went at his loving like a starving woman.

"A little, but I'm not complaining."

"I'm not either. Not even over the small scratches on my back."

Winter hopped down from the high bed and walked over to him, anxious to check his back to see what she'd done. She hurried in helping him get his coat and sweat shirt off.

"Oh, my goodness. I am so sorry."

"Baby, don't," he said taking both of her hands into his.

"I have missed how zestfully you love on me. It felt good; still does. My body can handle it. Question is, how did your body handle mine? I saw you wince when you got down from the bed. You need a good, hot soak. You were telling the truth about not being with anyone. That tightness was real and oh, so delightful, which we both know sent me surging like a madman. Trust me, only for you."

When Dante pulled her into his embrace and found her lips. she exhaled and took all that he offered. She missed being kissed this lovingly and thoroughly.

"Massage of your leg and then breakfast?" she asked.

Dante looked her over and then down to the juncture between her legs.

"Massage after breakfast. Do I get to choose the meal?" he asked with sexual exuberance.

"I guess I don't have to ask Santa if you're being naughty or nice."

"I'm naughty and nice. Want to find out in the shower?"

She loved that he didn't wait for her answer. She giggled when he picked her up and walked them into the trailer's shower. She was more than ready for his version of breakfast.

Nine

"There's a space over there," Winter pointed.

Pepper leaped up from her space on Winter's lap and looked out of the window. It was clear she was excited to be out as much as she and Dante were.

"Good looking out. I was about to drive around again," Dante said before turning the truck and getting a parking spot on the large lot where another car was pulling out of.

"You know, you had a great idea coming out to see all of the holiday decorations around town and then coming here to the town's holiday festival. I can't wait to get a cup of hot chocolate."

Pepper barked at them.

"Oh, you look so cute in your Christmas sweater. Where did you get this for her?" she asked Dante.

"I have quite a few of them. There is a shop, which we'll walk by in a minute, that has a lot of sweaters and other cold weather stuff for fur family members. About a year ago, a few months after I first got her from a pet rescue center in Chicago, I was here. There is an entire drawer in the trailer that belongs just to her. She has quite the wardrobe."

"That is hilarious. I didn't know men did things like that. Usually, women dress their fur babies up."

"I can't say I dress her up all the time, but in the winter, I make sure I keep her warm. Sometimes she hates it. Today, she didn't put up a fuss. I think she knew we were going to do something fun and she didn't want to be left behind. Since I knew we would be walking around outside tonight, I picked the warmest sweater I have for her. Won't matter much. She'll walk a little bit because she'll be excited about all the kids. She'll give me a look when she's ready for me to pick her up. I carry a small blanket when I take her out at night for just that reason. Can you reach behind my seat and grab it?"

"Of course. We have to keep her warm."

Winter grabbed the blanket and talked to Pepper until Dante came around and opened her door. She handed Pepper to him as she stepped out. Dante immediately placed Pepper on the ground after putting her leash on. They laughed when Pepper tried to take off without them.

"Told you. She loves the bright lights, though, not so much the noise."

"How did you find out about this festival? For the past four days, we've been camped out either in the house or in your trailer. I almost forgot that there could be people around," she said humorously.

"Well, I figured we could use a night out. I also thought this would be a good time to give your body a rest from me. I haven't been able to keep my hands and other body parts off of you since that first night. I've become a drug addict off of your loving."

"I wasn't complaining about any of that loving. I wanted you just as much. I am happy about getting out tonight. I haven't been getting any work done anyway. Before you apologize, it's not your fault. Perhaps, I needed reminding that there is more to life. I've been enjoying your company until you kept beating me in Scrabble. I can't believe those old board games are still there."

"I remember where everything is. As a part of the exit survey guests fill out, I make sure they are being asked how we could make their stay more enjoyable. Surprisingly, a lot of the responses say they would like more board, card and family games. We've loaded the house up with them. We'll play something different later on, if you would like."

Winter placed her hand in Dante's hand that he extended out to her as they walked toward the bright festivities.

"I'd like that. I do love board games. The Christmas decorations around town have gotten much more extravagant than what I remember years ago. People really go all out."

"That actually started last year with the new mayor. He instituted prizes around the best house decorations for various holidays. If you think Christmas is big now, you should see Halloween. I didn't get to be here for that but I saw pictures."

"Hello Dante. Is that Winter? Oh, my goodness. I haven't seen you in years. How are you?"

"Ms. Ethel?" Winter asked.

The woman had aged but she was definitely someone no one could forget. She was someone who lived full-time around these parts and had for many years.

"Yes, it's me, Ms. Ethel. It's good to see you again."

Before she could say another word, Ms. Ethel had her in a death hug, squeezing the life out of her. She always thought she gave the best hugs, but they sucked all the air out of your lungs. Anyone on the opposite end would have to remember to hold their breath for a few seconds as she had quickly done.

"Oh, dear. You are as beautiful as ever. I almost didn't recognize you with the hat, scarf and hood up. It is cold tonight. There will definitely be some snow later tonight. I hope you're ready for that."

"Yes, ma'am. I feel it in the air too."

"Last I saw you Dante, you mentioned you and Winter were divorced when I asked about her. Are you back together? If so, I think it's marvelous. I was married to my Harold for sixty-two years. Did I tell you we met when I was sixteen years old? We never would have gotten a divorce. I'm glad to see you patched things up. There isn't a couple more suited to live to sixty years of marriage like I did than the two of you."

"Mom, stop talking people to death. They like to keep moving to stay warm!"

"Is that Sonny?"

"Yes, that's my youngest son. He's visiting me for the month. The only one of my children who still hasn't found the love of his life. I brought him out tonight in hopes that maybe she's here in the crowd. Well, I better go before he screams for me again. Mr. Benson's shop has the best hot chocolate and cupcakes tonight. Stop there first. Merry Christmas. I am so happy to see you back together. Now, it's time to have a few kids and you'll be all set. No more divorce."

Dante looked to Winter who gazed his way in shock. They just had an entire conversation and barely said a word.

"She's still hilarious, I see," Winter noted as they walked in the direction of Benson's Bakery, a local favorite place this time of year.

"She thinks we're back together. You didn't say anything," Dante joked and raised her gloved hand to kiss the back of it.

"You didn't correct her either. I don't mind people thinking it if you don't. That's better than answering questions about us being divorced and now walking hand-in-hand. My mind was racing with how to respond to her. Didn't have to, so there's that. Her son saved us. Were you here last Christmas?"

"I was. I didn't stay at the house. It was already rented. I stayed at a campsite nearby. I think I was here about five days."

"What made you want to be here for a month this year?"

Winter had been wanting to ask a more in-depth question about his being here, but couldn't find the right time in all of their talks.

"I've been doing a lot of driving over the past few months. Pepper and I have really put some miles on the truck. I wanted to have a longer time being in one place. I love it here."

"I would love to hear about some of the places you've stayed during your travels that you really loved."

They walked into Benson's Bakery and found a table in the back. The one thing about most of the shops in town was that they were dog friendly. Dante couldn't have Pepper down on the ground inside so he had to have her in his arms at all times when indoors. She remembered him telling her that. When they sat, she immediately told Dante that she wanted a large hot chocolate, plain along with two cupcakes, one ginger cinnamon and the other red velvet. When he got up to order their food, she took Pepper and placed her on her blanket in her lap. After a few rubs behind the pup's ears, she was fast asleep. Her phone buzzed in her pocket. She started not to answer it, thinking it was one of her friends. She was still not speaking to them right now. They wouldn't understand her decision to be intimately involved with her ex-husband for the remainder of her stay. Each one of them would come up with hundreds of reasons why she would be making the biggest mistake of her life.

With her eyes on Dante where he stood in line waiting to place their order, she didn't have a care about what anyone thought. She was doing what she wanted to do and not what anyone else thought she should be doing.

For the past four days and especially nights, she and Dante had been enjoying the best and wildest sex of her life. She thought that first night on the edge of the bed with him standing on the floor and her behind over the edge gave her the best orgasm. The shower sex that morning with her back to his front and him loving her like never before from behind had her in her happiest mood in a long time all day long. The night before, she thought she wouldn't see him. He'd made plans, ahead of their sex agreement, to go visit a friend of his who was buying a lodge in the area. His friend wanted his advice on security measures to take. Him telling her about that had spawned a conversation about what he'd been doing in his travels. One of those things was consulting with various police and sheriff departments around the country. Though he didn't need the money due to his father's construction business that he'd sold along with other investments, money wasn't an issue. It was clear Dante loved what he had done in his career and wanted to stay close to it even if he could no longer be in the field.

Her eyes traveled down to his leg. He had only used the cane in the first few days after arriving. He'd found time to stop in to see a local physical therapist who checked on his leg. Doing that and the leg massages she loved giving him since they'd been spending time together, his leg hadn't been giving him any trouble. When her phone buzzed again, she pulled it out. Seeing Josie's name, she started to send the call to voicemail. Instead, she answered.

"If you're calling to pass more judgment, save it, Josie. I'm not in the mood."

"That's how you answer the phone when I call now? We haven't spoken in days. Are you still mad?"

"I am, but you already knew that. I'm trying to have a relaxed time and each of you want to start some drama. Don't you think I've had enough of that?"

Winter tried to whisper and not let the conversation anger her. She was enjoying her time with Dante.

"Did you forget that we were here when you cried every night after he left? We don't want to see you hurt again. You being there in Colorado while he's there isn't a good idea."

Winter sat up straight and stretched her shoulders. She looked down to be sure she didn't disturb Pepper. The pup was still sleeping and lightly snoring.

"Let me ask you a question. Are you with Cornell right now? For the holiday, aren't you with your part-time boo? Oh wait, what about Gabriel, the guy you call the Italian dynamo. And what about Davina? Isn't she wrapped around some male stripper somewhere? Dante and I are here at the same time. It is what it is. Y'all like to question anything that has to do with him as if I can't make my own decisions. I'm tired of it."

There was a long pause. Dante was ordering as she waited for more from Josie.

"You're sleeping with him. Tell me you are not spreading your legs for him again. *Winter?*"

She exhaled loudly. Not that she had to explain herself, but she decided to. She wasn't teenager trying to convince her mother that she was still a virgin.

"I am. So what?"

"What are you doing? I don't believe you. There are plenty of men out here who have been trying to get at you. You put all of them off. For what? To get back in bed with Dante? Why would you do that to yourself? You don't think there may be heartache at the end?"

"We're good together. We're here for a month. It's great sex. I know what it is. We're giving ourselves this month to just have some good fun. I intend to do that. If you are going to have anything to say that I'm not going to like, keep it to yourself. Stop meddling in my life. I don't tell you all the ways Cornell isn't good for you. We both know it. If you wanted to marry him, I may not like it but I would be the first to go with you to the bridle store. I'd be all smiles on your big day because I respect your choices, good or bad. Do that for me. I know you don't like Dante."

"No," Josie responded. "I love Dante. He's my brother. I don't like how he did you. I'm afraid he'll hurt you again. I don't want that for you or your heart."

"Let me worry about my heart."

Dante came back to the table and sat down.

"Just be careful. You're still in love with him. Is he still in love with you?"

Her eyes locked with Dante's. He blew her a kiss. She already knew.

"Yes. I have to go. I'll call you when I get back to L.A. I'm good for now. Bye."

Winter ended the call and placed her phone back in her pocket. She tried to hold her composure as she unwrapped one of the cupcakes. She knew the minute she'd made a mistake. She tore into that wrapper like it had done something to her.

"Winter? What's wrong? Who was that on the phone that completely destroyed your mood?"

She rested her hands on the table and re-situated Pepper on her lap.

"Do you want me to take her?"

"No, I have her. She's sleeping comfortable. I don't want to disturb her. I'm going to lift her up a little. Can you unfold the blanket some and put more of it around her fat little body. She is so adorable."

Knowing she was biding her time by having Dante help her, she took a deep breath before answering his question.

"Josie. That's who was on the phone."

"Oh? How is she doing?"

"She's fine. She's treating me like I can't make decisions for myself. I'm mad at all three of them right now."

"Why? Y'all are thick when it comes to friendship. What happened? Is it about me?" he asked.

"Kind of. They know you're here in Colorado. They think that I should have left when I discovered you were here too."

"Okay."

Dante's response was bland. She knew he was waiting for more information.

"I'm sorry. They can be a lot."

"They're your friends. Friends can be a lot sometimes. That shouldn't have you all not talking. What could they say that has made you so mad to the point of not talking to them?"

"When you left me and then divorced me, they were there. That was a really bad time for me. It was hard on me emotionally and mentally. They were concerned about the toll the divorce took on me. Their concern is that I would open myself up to being hurt by you again. I feel like they're judging me when I don't judge their choices, especially when it comes to me. You've been around. You know how supportive I have always been, even when they screw up. I'm an honest friend. I also understand that sometimes we may make choices that aren't good for us. Hopefully, there will be more days when we can get things right. None of us are perfect. I don't like how they seem to target my personal life and I don't like it."

"Don't let what is going on between me and you tarnish your friendship with them. That's not right. I don't want that for you. I agree that there have been times when I wished they would back off some when it comes to interfering in your life, but that's between you and them. They know how I hurt you. They don't know how much I still love you and would never, ever hurt you again. They're going by what they know. I can see then tension in your body after you were so relaxed when I went to place our order."

Winter relaxed her shoulders. She could feel the tension he noted."

"I know you miss talking to them. I thought it odd that I haven't heard you talk about them or talk to them. They love you. If I can understand how they feel, you have to. I messed up."

"True, but it's not their place to put out judgment and make me feel like lesser than I am if I'm not hating you for what happened. I don't want to hate you. I've never wanted that. I only wanted to understand. We've talked about that."

"Baby, look at me."

Winter stopped moving around and did just that.

"Dante, I don't want to be angry at anyone; not you and not them."

"Then fix it. You decide when. They don't know all of the things I've shared with you about my life at that time. What I went through as a husband not feeling like I could be still be that man for you. What losing S.W.A.T. did to me, only those closest to me know about that. What my injuries did to me was shattering to my spirit. It's not an excuse, but I know who I am now. They don't. Give them a little grace. If I can understand where they are coming from wanting to protect their friend, surely you can too. Now, get that smile and warm disposition back and let's enjoy these hot chocolates and cupcakes before Pepper wakes up and wonders why she doesn't have any."

Winter looked at him with a shocking, disappointed look on her face.

"You didn't get her anything?"

Dante laughed and showed her Pepper's doggy bag.

"Of course I did. This shop has the best doggie cupcakes. Pepper will get hers later when we go back. For now, we are having fun. We're going to check out all of the Christmas displays. There's going to be singing and marshmallows over open fires and best of all, there is Santa in the main square. Now, you can't get your picture taken with Santa Clause with a sad face."

"Of course not. I have to thank him for you being under my Christmas tree even if it's only for a month. It's been the best month that I've had in a long time. You know Christmas will always be my favorite time of year."

"Yes. There is something about the Christmas season that brings out the best in people, including me and you. I like that we've decided to enjoy this time; no confusion and no complications."

Dante took her hand and kissed the back of it. This time, she'd already taken her glove off.

"Let's go so that I can thank Santa and share with him everything else I want this year. He's on a roll so far!" Winter laughed.

"Me, too. I have a few additional wishes. You have no idea how thankful I am that you made that wish about me being under your tree. The result is happiness for me and you."

Ten

"Winter, while you're getting your shower, I'm going to take Pepper for a quick walk and then I'll go get her bed from the trailer since we're spending the night here in the house with you."

Dante yelled up the stairs inside of the house. He waited to see if Winter was able to hear him.

"Okay. If I'm done before you get back, do you want me to heat up the food we brought back with us? Those ribs and grilled chicken wings sure smell good."

"Yeah, we can eat when I get back. I won't be long."

He hadn't heard the shower start yet, so he knew he had time. He did cut the Christmas lights on around the cabin along with on the tree. Lighting the fire place, he then got Pepper up and out for her quick walk. When it's cold like it is on nights like this, he knew that Pepper liked to do her business and get back in out of the cold.

Being true to herself, that's exactly what she did. He had time to race into the trailer to get what they would both need. Within minutes, he was back in the house. He locked it up and set the alarms. With the heat on and the fireplace going, he quickly put a plan in place that he hadn't told her about.

Lucky for him, Pepper loved being entertained by movies

and of course snacks. He placed her timed-snack release tray on the floor at the end of the sofa. He moved her bed there and turned on his iPad to one of her favorite movies. With her relaxed for the evening, he knew he had to move quickly. He'd just heard Winter turn the shower off.

Moving quickly, he raced and grabbed a lightning speed shower in the first-floor bathroom. He didn't need to get fully dressed in evening attire. Instead, he quickly dried off and grabbed several pillows and four large blankets from the closet on the wall opposite the fireplace. He quickly placed two of the blankets on the floor in front of the Christmas tree. He placed the other two on the edge of the blankets he'd just placed.

"I'll be down in a minute," Winter yelled from upstairs.

"I'm ready for you," he said. Looking down his body at that part of him that stood out long, hard and ready for her, he grabbed his Santa hat, placed it on his head and laid down, completely naked on the blankets right near the tree. Making sure he was facing the stairs, he crossed his legs at the ankle and waited.

A few minutes went by before he heard Winter making her way to the steps. He leaned up on one elbow and waited for her to come get her Christmas wish. He didn't forget that she said she had asked Santa Claus if he could grant her a wish and place him under her Christmas tree. It wasn't Christmas morning yet. He still figured there was no time like the present to give her a surprise.

He loved the moment her eyes landed on him. Her surprised face turned to one of seductive temptation.

"Oh, I see you've got some shenanigans on your mind. I like. I like a lot," she said, descending the stairs and walking over to him.

Before he could fathom how to offer his own comeback, Winter had removed the red satin short robe. To his delight, underneath, she wore a very short red nightie that barely covered her large, chocolate brown breasts. He could see her nipples poking through the peekaboo lace front. From his place on the floor, he could look up and see that she was also naked underneath of it.

She came over to him smelling like peaches – another of her favorite aromas that he loved.

"I have an appetite tonight. Not that I don't want the food we brought back, but first, I want you to know that Santa Claus told me that I needed to plant myself right here under this tree. He wanted to be sure you were aware that he heard your wish and he didn't want to wait until Christmas morning for you to unwrap it," he kidded.

"Unwrap it? Baby, it looks like you did that part for me."

"Oh, no, sweetheart, there is this hat," he chuckled, pointing to it.

"You make gift unwrapping so easy."

Winter walked around until she stood above his body and looked down to that steely part of him that was pointed up in her direction.

Dante turned over onto his back and placed his clasped hands behind his head and wiggled his hips from side to side.

"I am to please."

"You are certifiable!" she boasted.

"I am certifiable in love and lust with you. I hear in these parts, when the weather is better, the locals like to ride horses. Care to come around these parts for a ride before dinner."

Winter licked her lips.

"You have a red hat on your head but nothing red on...the other head. I think I can remedy that. I happen to have on this bright red lipstick."

"I don't know if Santa's plan was for us to be this naughty under this tree when he told me to plant myself here."

"You're here now. You promised me you would be my wonderland. I'm feeling playing in the naughtiest of ways."

When Winter straddled his lap, he pulled her head forward and seized her mouth in a soul-stirring, body-stimulating kiss. He moved her body up a little in order to capture the hot skin of her sexy red laced covered mounds into his mouth. He captured first one nipple, teasing it with his tongue before placing little nips around it with his teeth. Holding both in his hands, he moved to the other one, giving it equal attention before lowering the straps to free them from their confining fabric. Winter's soft whimpers of pleasure drove him on. He loved her breasts. They were thick and soft and perfect for his mouth. Tasting them, one after the other, over and over, Winter used her body to allow his to playfully poke at her womanhood again and again. She didn't slide all the way down, but she teased him with her slick feminine heat.

"You feel so good gliding over me. You're really wet and dripping on me."

She kissed him this time, tugging on his bottom lip with her teeth, nipping at him just to raise the erotic level. She leaned close to his ear.

"Trust me, it's not from the shower."

Winter then kissed her way down his face, licking and sucking on his chin. As she moved further down his body with her breasts exposed and her little nightie showing just enough of area between her legs, he was ready to shoot off like a rocket and he wasn't even inside of any part of her body yet. Seeing her intentions, he realized where she was going.

When her lips caressed his chest and then down his stomach, her hand reached down and grasped his penis, he had a teeth-clenching need that tested his restraint like never before. This was about her and her wonderland.

His eyes locked on Winter's action as her mouth lingered above his erection. When she kissed the tip, his hips moved on their own, a hitch caught in his breath. He held himself back from surging into her mouth. Her pretty red lips made it hard in more ways than one.

As her hand stroked him from tip to base, going up and down as she continued to kiss and lick the tip of him. Still, he was holding on; barely and roughly.

When she took as much of him into her mouth as she could, Dante couldn't control his hips much at this point. Between her hands and her mouth working on him simultaneously, she was loving him into submission of anything she wanted and needed in life. He would give her the world just from the way her mouth felt on him.

On the pass of seeing himself disappear in her mouth, he growled in heat when her mouth went further and further down on him.

"Baby!" he shouted and encouraged her on with the gyration of his hips.

Winter quickened her movements until he could hardly hold onto the orgasm that had him teetering over the edge. Before he got there, he felt her move up his body. She planted her lower body right over his and sank down in a motion that stole his breath. She kissed him, flicking her tongue around his while her hips moved to take him fully into her body. When she threw her head back and began riding him, bracing her hands on his chest for leverage, he let her have her way. Winter getting what she wanted meant he would get the same as long as it included her never allowing him to leave the inside of her body ever again. She felt like home all soft, silking and sexy.

With ragged breaths, he held onto her hips as she bounced and twerked on him. Seeing her behind jiggle had his mouth watering. She rode him hard. She rode him continually. The only sounds in the air were of their bodies' liquid essence mixing and mingling.

Winter was a vision of beauty on top of him moving flawlessly like a goddess. Then her body shuddered and her thrusts became stronger. The shivers of her released stirred his on further. She had him experiencing an orgasm so strong and powerful that he'd never want to have one with any other woman again. Winter had claimed all of him once again.

She was gasping softly, shrieking with explosive screams while her arched back pumped faster and faster. He howled into the cozy open air of the room, giving her every single part of his body and soul. Her body devoured his. His body racked over and over, tearing him about in the most amazing way.

When the stars behind his eyes finally released him and Winter's limp body collapsed onto his, her breaths strained, he held her to him.

"If I died right now, I would do so as the happiest man on the planet," he was finally able to stumble out.

Winter went between kissing his cheek and his neck while he pulled one of the blankets over and covered their bodies.

"You can't do that yet. You promised me until the end of the month."

Dante's body heaved with laughter and he pulled her close.

"That was incredible. You move those hips masterfully. I erupted like a volcano."

"I felt you. I still feel you. The flashes of heat and fire throughout my body allowed me to have an out of body experience tonight. I've wanted this all day. Thanks for being under my tree. You are full of surprises," she said.

"Wait until my next trick!" Dante declared.

Eleven

Winter paced around the family room in the cabin while she spoke with her team who all joined her on their last production call of the year. They were five days before Christmas and working to wrap up ideas for the next season of her hit show, *Girls' Trippin'*.

"Okay, so the next season will have four new girls. We closed out the love lives of the four women from series one. Jamilla from season one will join three new ladies for this new season. That will allow us to bridge the two seasons together. This trip is about the ladies heading off to a new destination, Silent Whisper resort on the private island in the Mediterranean that's owned by the Blackstone brothers, Tellum, Byrum and Callum. I believe this is the one that Byrum oversaw the development of. The location is perfect for the time we want the women to have. Have any of you seen the photos of those resort rooms that are built into the side of the mountain? Gorgeous. Just gorgeous."

Winter was excited that she got word that the final contracts were all signed and they had the green light to begin production in the summer.

She heard cheers on the other end from everyone on the zoom video call.

"I can't believe we get to go to the island. This is so exciting!" Bridget, one of her production assistants cheered.

"Yes, everyone here on this call will be onset. According to their lawyer, Adrian Jarreau, they are making accommodation assignments for everyone after consulting with me on who should be where. I wanted to have this call, ahead of Christmas, so that we could celebrate this massive achievement. This has been in the works since we started on the first season. I wanted a different location and four new storylines. Though we have the storylines in place, it will seem more real once we're able to tour the island in order to make the script come to life with actual visuals."

"Winter, are you still in Colorado? When are you coming back? Also, no one wanted to ask but your leadership team never said if we have the extra two weeks in January off."

"Yes. I am still in Colorado. You all have the extra two weeks off, with pay. You should plan to be back by January twenty-third. I'll be back in early March. I'm working on a movie I was asked to take up the mantle to write. I expect all of you to bring your thinking caps to the first meeting in January. I won't be there but the stars of the show will be there for their first read. I want to be sure we have the right combination of women who will be the best of friends. If they don't vibe, we'll need replacements. I don't want to keep any of you much longer. I called this meeting to go over some things. I know we've been on here for a few hours, so I'll let you go to get back to enjoying your time off. Have a great Christmas. Promise me you won't open your gifts until Christmas day. The only thing you got early were your Christmas bonuses."

"Which were very generous, Winter. Thank you for

negotiating those with the studio. We know there has been some pushback on costs," Tremell, another production assistant mentioned.

"True, but not for us. Season one was such a huge hit, that they want to see us happy. That not only means me and my contract, but for my team and all of your contracts as well. Now, everyone sign-off. Merry Christmas to you all and your families. Have a safe and happy new year!" Winter chimed.

After getting the same kudos from her team, she ended the video call.

"Are you hungry?" she asked Pepper who came running up to her. She picked her up and walked into the kitchen. She was glad that Dante wasn't here to see her carrying Pepper all over the house. He reminded her to not spoil her even though that's what he does every day.

"You have a gold necklace around your neck and your dad says I spoil you," she said, giving the pup a tight hug.

She sat her down near her food and water bowls while she got her lunch together. As soon as she finished, there was a knock on the door, followed by someone ringing the doorbell. She knew it couldn't be Dante because he has a key and the code to the door. He'd left earlier telling her that he had a few errands to run and would be back in a few ours. Four days ago, after a night of lovemaking under the tree, they'd spent time with old friends who were in Colorado at a local lodge. Later that night, they'd all gone dancing. That was something she hadn't done in a long time. She had a chance to learn some new line dances including the Baltimore line dance called, Bring in the Katz. She'd been wanting to learn the steps for a long time.

The next evening, they went to the movies where she felt

like a teenager again with a large box of popcorn, nachos with zesty cheese, a large soda that they shared and to satisfy Dante's sweet tooth, mounds of candy from the concession stand.

She got Pepper all set, who tackled the food like a starving pup.

"Your dad should be back soon. If not, I'll take you out for your walk while the sun is out. It's going to be extremely cold tonight. The three of us will snuggle up in front of the fireplace tonight to stay warm. You like that idea?" she asked, rubbing Pepper's back. Then she heard the doorbell again. She ignored it the first time since she wasn't expecting anyone. This time, she didn't. She felt okay checking to see who it was since it was daylight outside.

Racing to the door, she looked through the camera on the wall beside the door before opening it. What she saw couldn't be real. As if she were dreaming, she rubbed her eyes and even pinched herself. No way was this real. When yelling, shouting and screaming happened on the other side of the door, she flung it open to three open arms.

Davina, Josie and Tachina were standing on the porch ready to embrace her. The four of them screamed with delight and pulled each other into one large hug.

"Oh, my goodness! You're here? The three of you are here? How?" Winter yelled.

"Your man invited us. We came immediately. Girl, he even paid our way! We missed you and hated not talking to you," Josie explained.

With their foreheads all touching, Winter cried out her happiness at seeing her three best friends.

"I missed y'all so much. I'm sorry for not talking to you.

I'm so sorry."

"We're sorry too. We love you, Win. This house is amazing. Is there any heat inside?" Davina said.

"Yeah, because we are freezing our warm weather asses off our here. Damn, it's cold!" Tachina said.

"Oh, I'm sorry. Get in out of this cold."

Winter looked beyond them to see Dante coming up on the porch carrying suitcases.

"Hi, baby," he said, quickly greeting her with a kiss before taking everything inside.

"But, how? How did you plan this? You did this? You brought them here?" she asked when they were all inside.

"They're your friends. I called Josie who put all three of them on a call. We talked things out. I told them about what that time was like for me and what I went through."

"Girl – we had no idea. By the end of the call, he had us all crying over the struggle he must have gone through. We didn't know. We are so sorry for judging either one of you. You know we didn't mean it. We love you," Josie explained.

Winter gathered with the three of them again and they shared a large group hug.

"It's okay. It's water under the bridge at this point. We are being positive. You're my sisters and I love you. How long are you staying? We have so much to catch up on."

"You look happy. You look good too. We'll be here for two days, until the twenty-third."

"So, you all just hopped on a plane and decided to come. You didn't have anything else going on? Work? Nothing?"

"After Dante called and told us that he felt like you needed us, we dropped everything. He didn't like the idea that he was the cause of us not speaking to each other. We didn't like it either. He wanted us to fix things. He said if we could get away, he would cover the expense. He made the arrangements and picked us up at the airport. Love the truck, by the way, Dante," Davina exclaimed.

"I forgot how nice this house was. I see a lot of new touches," Josie said, looking around.

Winter found Dante observing their excitement from the door.

"We're going to have a good time over these two days," Tachina said. "Remember Sabrina who works with me? Girl, she's pregnant by Julius!" she added.

"Wait, isn't Julius married?" Winter asked.

"Yes. To another woman in our office! Drama!" Tachina offered.

"Ladies, I'm going to leave you to your good time," Dante said, interrupting the start of their girl gossip-fest.

"You're leaving?" Winter asked, walking over to him.

"This is your time with your friends. You know where to find me. Where's Pepper? We'll get out of your hair."

"We're going to go look around. Is that okay? It's been a long time since we've been here," Josie said.

"Yes. Take a look around," Winter said and then turned back to Dante.

"You're going to have a blast. Pepper and I are going to relax in the trailer and catch a movie. I've ordered a heap of food for you all. It'll be delivered in about an hour. Food, snacks, sweet stuff and a special delivery from the liquor store. Have fun with your girls. I know you miss them. Make up. Do all the things you girls do. They forgave me. Don't keep punishing them for caring enough about you to not want to see you leap into anything with me. I told them at the end of the month, they get you back and they won't have to worry about me messing up your life."

Winter moved into his arms and held on when he wrapped his arms around her body.

"You're not messing up my life. I'm enjoying being with you."

"We are enjoying each other. For the next two days, enjoy your girls and if you need me, you know where I'll be."

"You did this for me. Thank you, Dante. Until I saw them today, I didn't realize how much I missed them. I was being difficult."

"You're not anymore."

Before they could finish talking, Pepper wandered, in her slow walk kind of way, over to them and right up to Dante.

"She missed you. I'm going to miss you."

"I'm always where you need me to be. I'm in that door right over there."

Dante kissed her sweetly before rubbing her behind, a gesture she loved. His love language was definitely touch.

"Girl! What are we going to do tonight?" Josie asked coming down the steps from upstairs level.

Winter closed the door behind Dante after she watched him and Pepper go inside of the trailer.

**

Even though the hour was late, Dante heard the trailer door open and knew who it was. He checked the time. It was after one in the morning. It was now clear to him that Winter loved the late-night hours. He was splayed out on the bed watching his favorite rerun of shows of Blue Bloods. Pepper was in her bed, this time at the front of the cabin. He'd left the under-cabinet lights on the light up the floor if she decided to come to the back; which she did sometimes. Tonight, he was glad he'd left them on. Winter was here.

"You're here. What's wrong?" he asked after Winter locked the door and petting a sleeping, Pepper.

"Nothing is wrong. I couldn't sleep."

"Are the girls asleep?" he asked.

"They are drunk sleep. I haven't seen them down that much wine in a long time."

Dante moved over the moment Winter walked over, kicked off her brown UGG boots and her robe and climbed up in the bed in a pair of Christmas pajamas. She snuggled next to him.

"Why couldn't you sleep?"

"Because I've gotten used to being in this bed or the bed in the cabin with you. I like how warm and toasty you are. I was missing you."

"How much did *you* drink tonight?"

He could smell the wine. From the little bit of lighting, he could see from her eyes that she'd had a few.

"A few glasses a wine. Maybe a daiquiri or two. I don't remember," Winter said and yawned into his chest.

"Get some sleep, baby. You have a full day of fun with your girls. You have the spa and shopping."

"I know and I can't wait. Right now, I just want to enjoy being in your arms. What are you watching?"

"Blue Bloods."

"Your favorite show. Are you still sad it's not coming back with new episodes."

"Very, but it's all good. Do you want to watch something else?"

Winter didn't answer. He looked over at her and she was

already fast asleep. He wrapped her tighter in his arms and pulled the blanket up around her shoulders. Kissing her forehead, he was already wondering how was he going to be able to get back to his life at the end of the month. Them like this, together is all he wanted. If it were up to him, they would be married again before the end of the year. He lost her once and didn't want to suffer through that again because they were going back to their lives and living them separately.

In the quiet of the night, he whispered his own wish to Santa Claus. The idea of it was silly, but he remembered his mother once told him, as a little boy, to never stop believing in the power of a wish, especially at Christmas time. That's when the power of love is most active. He loved Winter. He wanted to be her forever wonderland again. If he could get that, he would never take her for granted again.

He turned the television off, turned their bodies so that he could spoon with her.

"I've always loved you and I always will. I'm not whole without you. I love you, baby."

He pulled her even closer, wrapping the comforter tighter around them. After placing a soft kiss on the back of her neck, he settled in thinking about how perfect this moment with her was. Should he tell her that for Christmas, coming up in two days that all he wanted was her? It had to be her. He'd put his heart in every second they spent together. Everything he relayed verbally and, in his actions, told his truth about not wanting to be away from her. yes, she hadn't done the same. At least, not in the way that he had. Could she really walk away after the month they've shared? If so, he couldn't blame her if she couldn't let go of what happened before. Over and over, he'd told her how much he still loved her. He could tell by the look in her eyes several times that she wanted to say it. He gave her grace. Being open with him again and the not knowing had to be hard. Time. If he had to wait a lifetime for Winter, he would.

Dante closed his eyes. In seconds, he was asleep, imagining what life could be like if she just gave him another chance at loving her right.

**

Winter heard him. She heard his expression s of love, and not for the first time in the past month. Her mouth struggled to express what was in her heart. He held her tight in his arms. She'd never felt more at home than she did right now. Her head was a little foggy from the wine, but she knew what her mouth wanted to say even if Dante couldn't hear it because his light snoring told her he was fast asleep. She said it anyway.

"I love you, too."

She then joined him in slumber.

Twelve

Not a good day. Winter repeated that over and over. She was not having a good day. So far, besides packing, all she could seem to do was cry.

She thought about how long she'd not only been packing to head back to Los Angeles in the morning, but also, how long she'd been heavily crying with tears that flowed steadily. With each piece of clothing she packed after washing and drying everything earlier in the day, additional tears blurred her vision. She'd spent one hell of a month and just like that, it was coming to an end. If she had to compare it to other months, December would go down in history as one of the best months of her entire life. At this moment, it was also one of the saddest. She hated seeing the end of the month come so fast. Time slowing down before today would have been a great idea.

She wiped her eyes on the sleeve of her pink turtleneck shirt before reaching for the basket filled with her last load of laundry. Dumping it out on the bed, she started going through it and folding items before placing them in one of her three suit cases. She paused when a familiar shirt came into view. Remembering when she got the shirt made her cry harder. Even though no one was in the house but her, she put her hand over her mouth to stifle her uncontrollable sobs. She wasn't ready.

When her phone vibrated on the bed next to the clothes, she moved them and checked the screen.

"Not now, Josie," she yelled.

The last thing she wanted was for any of her friends to hear her crying. Her mood wasn't the best for conversing. She let the phone ring. When it finally stopped, she breathed a sigh of relief until it started ringing again. No doubt, she wasn't going to be able to avoid Josie. This was her last night in Colorado. She expected all of them to call to be sure she was prepared to head out the next day. She wasn't. Them knowing her truth wasn't the topic she wanted to discuss.

Knowing the calls would continue, she grabbed the phone and wiped her eyes some more.

"Were you ignoring me or you didn't have your phone with you?"

"I'm packing to leave tomorrow."

The sound of her own voice speaking the words out loud was a lot. She tried to inhale to hold in her cries, but she couldn't. She hid it well.

"Last night. Is Dante still there or did he leave already?"

Winter walked around to the other side of the bed and looked out of the window at Dante's trailer. A few hours ago, she watched from this very window as he hitched his trailer back up to his truck. Tomorrow, after saying their goodbyes, he would drive out of her life once again. The idea of that was frustrating. The last thing she wanted was to be apart from him again. Her love was too great. Their love was too great. Though they each knew it, no one made a move toward something other than going in two different directions. He had left it up to her. Fear was keeping her from her fight this time.

When she finally opened her mouth to reply, no words came out – only cries from a place deep in her belly.

"He's leaving me, again," she bellowed.

She moved and sat down on the edge of the bed. Her left leg tapped on the floor. Her body began to shake.

"Oh, babe. I hear you crying. No. What happened?"

Winter cried even harder. Josie tried consoling her but her cries wouldn't stop. Talking about it made the reality a sure thing.

"I don't want to go. I don't want to go without him. I love him, Josie."

"Hon, you always have."

"No, Josie. This is different. The way we connected over this month was more than the years we spent married to each other. I understand why he left me before. I don't know how I'm going to be able to let him go a second time."

"Then don't. What's stopping you? Please stop crying. I'm not close enough to give you a sisterly hug; the kind you need right now. Take some deep breaths. I haven't heard you cry like this since..."

Winter cut her off.

"Since he left me two years ago. I know. I cried like this after that. Today, I feel like I can't breathe. This month was everything. Christmas Eve and Christmas day were perfect. We cooked a big meal together. Somehow, we were able to buy each other small gifts without the other knowing it. We popped popcorn and watch Pepper tear through the paper of her wrapped gifts. We at sweet potato pie right out of the tin with one fork; not each, one fork. We fed each other. The moment was perfect. Dante and I shut the world out and connected like never before. I love him so much. He's leaving without me tomorrow. I don't know if I can handle that twice. It's hard breathing thinking about going back to my life without him."

"How does he feel? Do you know? Did you ask him?"

"He wants me."

"Then what's wrong? He wants you. We all saw that when we were there with you. He couldn't take his eyes off of you. You told us that after we left, the two of you spent every night together either in the house or in the trailer. Now, you're leaving and the idea of the emptiness is overwhelming."

"Yes. You got it. I don't know what to do."

"Winter! Stop this right now. You know exactly what to do. Dante knows he hurt you; it was bad. He never stopped loving you. You didn't stop loving him. You're in this together, but you're willing to keep doing this thing called life apart. You don't have to. He left it up to you to decide what would be next for you. Do you think he's not hurting the way you are right now? I bet he is. That man doesn't want to leave you. He has put his heart all out there. He's waiting to see if you're going to forgive him enough to try again. Are you willing to let your heart trust that he will never leave you again?"

"Yes. I know he won't."

"What the hell are you crying about then? Go get your man. Go tell him that you release him from what happened in the past. You asked Santa to put that man under your tree and he did. He did so in a mighty way. Yet, here you are still questioning yourself. You were willing to kick us to the curb because we questioned your long-lived love and desire for a man who walked away from you. We forgave him. I know you have forgiven him. Now you have to forgive yourself and get what you want most. What do you really want? Tell me," Josie said.

Winter heard the seriousness in her voice. Yes, she had her doubts. Still, she wanted to give her and Dante another chance. She can't do that if she's in Los Angeles and he's traveling the country in his trailer.

"I want my husband back."

"Good. Then in the spirit of this Christmas season, go have a happy, merry and delightful life with your man. Go get him, girl!"

Winter stood and wiped her face clear of all tears. She looked out of the window again and saw the lights on inside. It was getting late but not too late to go see him.

"Josie, I love you, sis. I'll call you back."

"You better. I need to know if your plans are changing."

"I promise, I will call you back. Thanks for your support. I knew what I needed to do. I just needed your shove. You're good at that."

"I love hearing it. Get off the phone!" Josie yelled.

Winter threw her phone to the bed and raced for the steps. She didn't even bother to grab her coat though it was ten degrees outside. She didn't care. She had to try and get her forever back.

Thirteen

Dante was just about finished cleaning up the trailer cabin in preparation for his road trip tomorrow where he'll be heading to Florida when he heard loud and incessant pounding on the door. He was in the back of the trailer. Thinking something must be wrong, he rushed to the front with Winter in mind. He was barefoot in a pair of jeans and a black t-shirt. He would run out as he was if something was wrong with her.

Quickly unlocking the inside steel door, he found Winter on the other side of the outside storm door in clothing but no coat. It was freezing out. Something had to be wrong. The moment he saw her face, his mind went into protective mode. She'd been crying. With the outside door unlocked, Winter pulled on the door handle hard, swinging the door open as far as it would go. When she looked up at him from the ground, down the three steps up, he started moving toward her when she leaped up the steps in his direction. He had to move back to give her room. She was breathing raggedly, frightening him.

"Baby? What the hell is wrong?" he excitedly asked while also looking around outside of the trailer to see if there was danger nearby that had her running out in the freezing cold. He'd barely got the last word out when she leaped up into his arms, barely giving him time to catch her.

Winter threw her arms around his neck and held on tight. When she placed her head against his neck and cried out like she was in pain, he held her close. Pepper raced to them and barked up at her. Even she could sense Winter's pain.

"I...I..."

That was all she said; that one letter. It was clear she was crying too hard to say anything else.

"Are you hurt? Injured? Is someone after you? What's wrong? What's going on? You're scaring me, Winter. Talk to me, baby."

He held her tight while pulling her even closer. With her legs wrapped around his waist, he didn't have to hold her up. Instead, he focused on trying to calm her down by caressing her back with both hands making soft circles on her back.

"Is there someone outside?" he asked moving toward the opened door.

Winter shook her head no. With her safely in his arms, if something or someone was out there, he quickly shut the door, locking them inside together. He was close enough to the box where he kept two weapons, a pistol and a rifle if he needed them. Until she spoke, all of his senses were activated. His mind and eyes were everywhere.

"No one is out there. I'm okay," she finally stammered out.

She leaned back and wiped her face with hand. He used one of his hands to wipe the other side of her face.

"Talk to me. I thought I was going to have to shoot someone. What gives?"

Winter again held him around his neck and spoke into it.

"I want us; I want you. I don't want to be apart from you. I don't want us living two different lives again. I hated it. I hated not being with you for the past two years. After this month, I can't do it again. I don't want to."

Dante exhaled. Until she finally spoke, he was practically holding his breath waiting to hear what had her troubled enough that she was not only crying buckets, but she raced to him in the freezing cold without protections from it.

"You don't have to. You already know that. What did I tell you? What's next for us is up to you. I wouldn't dare take it for granted that you wanted me from this point on as much as I want you. I'm yours. You never have to question that."

Dante reassured her not just with his words, but with the kisses he splayed all across her face from her chin to her forehead before his lips finally rested on hers. When she continued to cry even while kissing, he deepened it to make sure she knew that his promise to be here if she wanted him was his truth. She wasn't in this love alone; never again.

"I love you."

"You are crying because you love me?" he smiled and asked.

With her head back in the crook of his neck, he could feel her lips turn up into a smile.

"I couldn't breathe knowing that you are leaving tomorrow. You're leaving without me. I'm supposed to go back home. How could we end up here again – going our separate ways?"

"We? We?" he asked twice. "There is no we in us going in different directions. I told you that first night we made love right here in this trailer that I wanted you. It wasn't about the sex. It was about you and me making the biggest mistake of my life two years ago. All I needed to know is what direction you wanted to go in and I would take it from there. I love you, baby. There is no one else in this world for me but you; not ever again. I want us. Do you want us?" he asked.

Winter nodded and leaned back. They were again eye to eye.

"You can't leave here without me."

"Then I won't. What do you want me to do?" he asked.

"I want to go with you and Pepper."

"To Florida?"

"Yes. I don't have to be back in Los Angeles until mid-February. I was going to visit my family for two weeks and then head back home. It's lonely there without you."

"Your words are exactly what I need to hear. I didn't have a plan. I hoped and prayed and even asked Santa to speak to your heart so that you would give us another chance. I didn't fight for us the first time. I will forever fight for us from this point on. Are you sure you want to be on the road with me and Pepper? It's a long ride to Florida. We'll be camping out along the way to take in the sights. Pepper loves that. She also loves you. Well, not as much as me, but she does," he joked.

"I love her too. Mostly, I love you. I get it. I forgive you. We had to go through the past two years alone in order to appreciate the chance to give it another try."

"I won't mess up again."

"Did Santa answer you?" Winter asked him.

"He sure did. How do I know? Because you are right here in my arms. We're going to figure out what tomorrow will look like. I say we get up, take your truck back to the airport and then cancel your flight plans."

"That's a great start. Is there enough room in here for all three of us?"

"After the days and nights you've already been in here, you're still asking that? There is more than enough room."

"That's good because I have come to love this trailer. I never saw this for me, but I'm already loving the idea of it."

"Next, we'll pack your things and move everything to the trailer."

"I like that. Then?"

Winter looked at him with that look in her eyes that says she wanted to seal all of their decisions in the best way possible. The idea of it made him instantly hard for her.

"We'll have plenty of time for that."

"Oh, you're no fun. Then what else did you have in mind?"

"We'll get on the road tomorrow, as planned and head to see my mother in Florida. She will love to know that we are us again."

"I think my parents will be too. I'm going to call them tomorrow."

"Good idea because our parents need to know that we're getting married."

The moment Winter's body stiffened, he waited to see her reaction to that next part of his plan for them.

"Married? Did you say we're getting married? Again?"

"I love you. I want to marry you again. We never should have gotten a divorce. I will never make that mistake again. First, I need to correct the one I made two years ago. Will you marry me? Again?"

"Yes!"

He laughed at her.

Hearing her accept boisterously and exuberantly without hesitation surprised him. He thought he'd have to beg for days before she accepted.

With excitement on a whole other level, he spun them around in the small space near the door.

"Yes, baby! We'll get a ring while we're on the road. I hope we won't have to wait forever to actually do it. I need you to be Mrs. Eastman much sooner than rather."

Winter paused and slid out of his grasp to the floor.

"I've always been Mrs. Eastman. I never changed my name back."

"But you asked for that in the divorce decree. You wanted to go back to Shaw."

"I started using Shaw because I've always used it for work. On paper and legally, we are divorced but my last name is still Eastman."

"Well, that makes life a lot easier. I want to remember this as the best Christmas ever. It's the year I got my love back. Do you think it was Santa making our individual wishes come true?" he kidded.

"I think it was his plan all along. Santa had us end up at the cabin at the same time. He knew we had to slow down in order to find each other again. I don't care what we do, where we live – hell, I'll take living in your trailer for one hundred, Alex!"

They laughed out loud together.

"You have a career while I don't. What life looks like for us is up to you."

"You're the rich one," Winter reminded him.

Truth was, he was well off enough that he wouldn't have to work if he chose not to. He would still be able to take care of her for as long as they lived. His priority was being with her until the end of time."

"You love your career. The world loves your career. Our life will follow you. I'll figure something out for me. What do you say we get some dinner while we finish packing for tomorrow? I want to get on the road first thing."

"I'm excited. Just you, me and Pepper on the open road living like nomads. How spontaneous of us. That is until life becomes real again and it's back to Los Angeles."

Dante picked her up in his arms again and spun them around.

"With me in tow. Before I forget, remind me to call Rhea at the property management company so that I can thank her for her minor mishap. That error has changed my life for the better. She has no idea that because of her, I have my wife back. My heart is officially right back where it should be; entwined with yours inside of your chest. Thanks for starting over with me."

"My wonderland, just remember that this is our lesson that we were always meant to be. Let's get dinner so that we can get back here and make love all night."

Dante loved the sound of that.

"My place here or yours over there?" he asked pointing to the house.

"I would say in the middle but that would put us outside in the cold."

Dante chuckled.

"I do have camping equipment if you really want to be risky and frisky!"

"I'll take no thanks for one thousand Alex!"

"Oh yeah, you are a Jeopardy fan."

"Camper it is, since we're already here. We can get comfortable and order food to be delivered. In the meantime, I'm wondering if we can start on that lovemaking part."

Winter started removing clothes before he could get the last word out. He whistled which each piece that she removed and tossed his way.

"I'm a step ahead of you with that."

"This month will go down as the best trip of my life! You are absolutely the most amazing Christmas gift a man could ask for," he declared before quickly matching her nakedness.

"I love the sound of that. How about the best ride of your life?"

"Oh, I'll take that. I hear there is a rodeo in town. Giddy up, baby!"

Epilogue

The only sound in the cabin in Colorado was that of the fireplace crackling. Winter sat on the sofa across from it with her legs crossed at the ankles as they rested on the large plush fleece ottoman. She was as content as any woman could ever be. Her hands went from caressing Dante's bald head then down to his thick black with specks of gray goatee and beard. There could never be a more perfect scene before her than to watch the strongest man she's ever known coo and whisper to their soon-to-be-born daughter. Winter watched and felt Harleigh Renee, the name Dante had already picked out for her ahead of her arrival in three months, move around in her belly. A few minutes before, Dante had begun singing, everybody was Kung Fu fighting! Harleigh was busy today.

"Are you nice and warm in there?" Dante spoke whispered against her stomach.

Winter stifled her outburst of laughter. He'd been doing this for the past thirty minutes. Truth be told, since the moment she told him that she was pregnant, besides overwhelmingly loving her, he's been filled with anticipation of the baby's birth by talking to her every day. He wanted Harleigh to know his voice and how much she is loved even before she arrives.

"She is as warm as you and I are in front of this fireplace. Can you believe how quiet the house is? A few hours ago, between your mother and my mother making all the plans for the baby shower, to my father and my brother-in-law play fighting over a game of chess, this place was filled with chatter and laughter."

"I'm glad everybody made it to Colorado this Christmas. A year ago, it was just you and me, unexpectedly rekindling our love. I'm surprised we beat them here. We drove the trailer from California. We beat everyone by a day. I still can't believe you didn't want to fly," Dante reminded her.

"Fly? Me? Absolutely not while in this condition. Besides, I wanted to relax while you chauffeured me, Harleigh and Pepper."

"Harleigh? Did you hear that? Your momma is still controlling everything, including how we travel. That is, until you get here. At that point, all bets are on you being in control of both of us," he added.

Winter giggled louder when he kissed her stomach where their daughter was poking a fist out that actually hit Dante on the cheek.

"Our little boxer. She's wrestling around in here like she's fighting her way out," Winter kidded.

"I can't wait until she gets here. We have had some year since this time last year. I mean, you and your show were not only nominated for a second year with six Emmy awards; you actually won all six, including outstanding writing for a comedy series for *Girls' Trippin'*. That was all you. To think we are back here where our life started all over again. Our life together has been uphill since then. You have had an incredible year in work and in love. Oh, don't let me forget that you were tapped to write the next big screen black romance movie. People are saying it will be bigger than *Love Jones* and *Love and Basketball* put together. That movie trailer is all the buzz in and out of Hollywood. Great year, indeed," Dante said celebrating her.

Winter leaned down and kissed his forehead. She loved how he never stopped being her biggest supporter. She had a few celebrations about him as well. Dante has come a long way from where they were after they split.

"I'm not the only one who had a great year. After leaving here last year, we got married a month later. We settled into a new home in Los Angeles a few months ago in preparation for the baby coming. You accepted a role back with S.W.A.T. as the senior officer in the department's Special Operations Bureau. It's not out in the field but you are the glue that holds your old team together while preventing any of them from getting into situations that could mean life and death for them. You fight for them the way you've always wanted to. You're in a position where they have to listen to you. Your teams are stronger than ever. Being in charge looks good on you. Besides that, you seem happy. You are happy, right?"

Dante sat up and took her hand into his.

"Baby, I don't think I've ever been happier than I am right now. I loved being on the streets with a team. Being Commander Eastman is so much better. I can make a difference in the lives of all S.W.A.T. members. As for us, I thought I was happy the first time we married, but this time around is more than any man could ever ask for. We are still growing together."

"You're more patient," she offered.

"That's new for me. I'm better because of it."

"We love intentionally without holding anything back," she added.

"There is never a time that I don't feel you in my corner," he noted.

"We put each other and our feelings first. Nothing comes before making sure that we'll always work through everything together."

Dante nodded and kissed her quickly.

"This life with you and my baby girl is all I need. Getting back here was a must. It's Christmas Eve, the decorations are up, especially the tree. Santa is still granting our hearts' desires. We're together. I know that we don't need a tree or even Santa Claus to give us what we want most, which is a continued life full of love and family. I like the idea of coming back for the sentimental value of it. I want to go through the motion each year by returning and making our plea to Santa for much more of each other at Christmas time to plan for the year ahead. Thank you for trusting me with your heart and the lives of my two favorite girls."

"I trust you with all of me and our daughter."

"And one day her sister and brother or plurals if that is what we want."

"Whoa, slow down cowboy. One baby at a time, but yes, as many as we want. I can't wait to be a mommy. I also asked Santa for that before we left last year. He came through on that end too."

Dante stood and pulled her up by her hands.

"Oh? He gets the credit for you being a mommy? Well, let's go out to the trailer, since the house is full with the family, including your sister's three kids. I want to give you a reminder, in private, of exactly what I did to make you a mommy. I don't know if you should howl like you tend to do. It may scare the family when all of the animals in the woods show up here after hearing your mating call!" he joked.

Winter grabbed their coats and shoes near the door while Dante put out the fireplace and turned off all of the Christmas lights. As much as she always desired her husband, being pregnant has taken her need to a whole new level of want.

"I can't make any promises. Pepper may not get any sleep, though. You know how crazy I've been for your touch since this whole pregnancy thing started."

"You don't have to tell me. I'm extremely happy to oblige my beautiful wife. This is my happiest Christmas ever. I would do anything for you. With the help of the Christmas spirit, you have your winter wonderland back. Feel free to play all day and all night. I am and always have been your playground."

After putting on their shoes and coats, Winter grabbed Dante by his coat collar and pulled him out of the front door of the cabin and toward the trailer. She growled at him in that sexy manner that he liked.

"I'm ready to ride right into Christmas morning. I love you, my wonderland!" she purred.

"I love you, my forever Christmas wish."

**

Thank you in advance for leaving a review. Independent authors count on them to help us reach new readers.

A Christmas holiday romance coming soon

His Holiday Wife – December 17, 2025

Lance Barrett was set to marry a woman his family predicted and his boss expected in order to keep up with the image of a powerful corporate executive.

His fiancé Angelique Gates was too busy or simply not interested in meeting his family over the Christmas holiday season. He wasn't sure which was true when she came up with a stand-in bride-to-be, a barista, Maia Dutton, whom she considered not in his or her league, to accompany him for two weeks in the small Mississippi town.

What Lance didn't expect was for Maia to show him what he was missing when it came to the true meaning of family over image for Christmas.

~~Recent Release~~
Never Can Say Goodbye

Book publisher, Taryn Novack, who lives in Paris, has lost more than she loved, and she's had enough of saying goodbye. When she finally gets a chance to be close to unapologetically sexy attorney, Adrian Jarreau, it wasn't the best of circumstances. She had fallen at his feet and when she looked up, she got more than she bargained for. He was in a towel, and nothing else.

Adrian has been secretly lusting after Taryn, the intriguing and stunning beauty who has captured his soul without knowing it. He feared that after their uncomfortable encounter, he would never get the chance to have her in his heart and in his bed.

Another loss in her family has brought Taryn back to New York and back to Adrian. What was an instant attraction for both may not be enough to never say goodbye again when a secret indiscretion from Taryn's past catches up to her. She fears it could destroy her life and newfound love with Adrian.

Is saying goodbye on the horizon again or can their love withstand a threat to her livelihood?

Connect with Cheryl Barton

Author Cheryl Barton website
www.cherylbarton.net
Amazon Author Page
www.amazon.com/author/cherylbarton
Instagram: @cherylbartonauthor
Facebook: @authorcherylbarton
Threads: @cherylbartonbooks@threads.net

More Holiday Romance Novels from Cheryl Barton

Home for Thanksgiving

Firefighter Nicholas Sullivan is going home for the holiday after he was sidelined due to an injury on the job. Guilt over a life lost has kept him away from his family's ranch in Montana and now he's forced to face his past demons and deal with a self-imposed life of regret.

Veterinarian Parker Wingate's first encounter with the ruggedly handsome firefighter was less than pleasurable. She sympathized with his hurt, understood his pain and before long, felt his love.

Knowing the holiday season is ending soon, can Nick go from living in love for the moment to allowing himself to finally live in love forever?

Read it now on Kindle Unlimited!

https://www.amazon.com/Home-Thanksgiving-Sullivans-Cheryl-Barton-ebook/dp/B01NACRPDD

Additional Christmas Romance Novels

Mister Christmas
A Christmas Wish
The Christmas Layover
Dashing Through the Snow
Holly for Christmas

Get them all at
www.cherylbarton.net

Hunger for You
Book 1 of the Island Embers series

Tellum Blackstone was entranced the moment his eyes landed on Cheyenne Reddick and her magnetic beauty. In her eyes, arms, and heart, he thought he'd found forever. A rift between their fathers had him questioning what kind of real love could be torn apart with a line drawn in the sand.

Cheyenne never thought that she would meet the perfect man until she did in Tellum. He exuded the kind of charm, kindness, and simmering heat that had her mind, body, and soul sizzling like no man had ever done before. To her dismay, a ticking time bomb of epic proportion, in the form of her father, brought about an ultimatum for her to choose a man she loves from a family he detests or lose his love and support forever.

At Secret Whisper, a romantic island resort owned by Tellum, Cheyenne finds that his passion-infused hunger for her easily penetrated her paper-thin resistance. Their desire for each other reignited an insatiable appetite that no woman in her right mind could fight.

Tellum put his all into their red-hot kisses and explosive days and nights of seduction. He needed to find a way to overshadow the risk they were taking in discovering if their love was worth fighting for.

Desire for You
Book 2 of the Island Embers series

Byrum Blackstone is considered the one Blackstone brother who could not be tamed by any woman, no matter how salaciously desirable she is. That is, until he finds himself vulnerable to the one woman he should stay far away from; his executive assistant, Keiko Lee.

In the midst of fighting for her freedom and for custody of her son, Keiko vows to never trust another man with her heart. What she didn't expect was for her boss to offer her wicked, blood pressure spiking, hotter than she's ever known before nights of passion that stir her body and her heart back to life.

Neither Byrum nor Keiko are willing to admit their true feelings as the bigger problem of losing their careers overshadows how bittersweet newfound love could be not just in the present, but in the foreseeable future.

Thirst for You
Book 3 of the Island Embers series

Callum Blackstone did the unforgiveable; he was caught with his ex-girlfriend by his girlfriend, Kendra Grimes. A year after their relationship ended, Kendra showed up asking for help for their twin boys that he didn't know he had. Putting their issues aside, they focus on getting their sons the medical help they need.

As they began to heal, Callum knew that in order to get Kendra back in his life so that he could be a full-time father to his sons, he had to work on a secret, quiet plan of love, adoration and untamed lust to get her to trust him again. There was no better place to do that than on the island of Hawaii at his new resort, Quiet Whisper. It was a magical place that anything wished for could be made true. He was counting on everlasting love being the end result.

Winning over Kendra's heart again wouldn't be easy. After leaving him once, love is what he hoped would bring her back to him in one of the most beautiful places in the world. He was up for the challenge because his thirst for her has never quenched.

www.ingramcontent.com/pod-product-compliance
Lightning Source LLC
Chambersburg PA
CBHW051843170626
46807CB00003B/1326